Love on the Rocks?

Charley stood beside Casey. "What happens if you stay here at Wilder?" he asked. "Won't you want your own boyfriend *here?* Won't you be lonely with me back in L.A.?—that is, if we stay together."

"I thought you just asked me to marry you," Casey said. "Now you're talking about breaking up?"

"I'm talking about what happens if you're here and I'm in L.A.," Charley said simply. "That's not going to be hard?"

"You think I can't handle a long-distance relationship?" Casey asked. "That I need to have someone near me all the time? That I probably think a Friday night date with some stranger is more important than the guy I love, even if he's far away?"

"I didn't mean it like that," Charley said.

"It sounds to me like you're the one who doesn't want a long-distance relationship," Casey murmured. "Maybe you're the one who doesn't like being single. Is that why you want to marry me? Too much temptation back in Hollywood?"

Nancy Drew on Campus™

Available from ARCHWAY Paperbacks

Nancy Drew
on campus™ #12

Just the
Two of Us

Carolyn Keene

AN ARCHWAY PAPERBACK
Published by POCKET BOOKS
New York   London   Toronto   Sydney   Tokyo   Singapore

AN ARCHWAY PAPERBACK *Original*

An Archway Paperback published by
POCKET BOOKS, a division of Simon & Schuster Inc.
1230 Avenue of the Americas, New York, NY 10020

Copyright © 1996 by Simon & Schuster Inc.
Produced by Mega-Books, Inc.

ISBN: 0-671-52764-9

First Archway Paperback printing August 1996

10 9 8 7 6 5 4 3 2 1

NANCY DREW, AN ARCHWAY PAPERBACK and colophon
are registered trademarks of Simon & Schuster Inc.

NANCY DREW ON CAMPUS is a trademark of
Simon & Schuster Inc.

Cover photos by Pat Hill Studio

Printed in the U.S.A.

IL 8+

Just the
Two of Us

CHAPTER 1

"Where *is* he?" Casey Fontaine wondered out loud, nervously raking her fingers through her short red hair as she stood in the lounge area of Suite 301 of Thayer Hall. Casey heard a door open and looked up to see Nancy Drew, one of her suitemates, coming down the hall wrapped in a bath sheet, wet strawberry blond hair tied back in a scrunchie.

"What time is it?" Casey asked her.

Nancy threw her a wry smile. "Since the last time you asked was *before* my shower, and now it's *after* my shower, I'd say it's a good ten minutes later. Which would put it at about ten thirty-seven and six seconds. But that's just a rough guesstimate," she said, and disappeared into her room with a grin.

"Funny," Casey deadpanned.

It was Sunday morning, and she'd been waiting for her boyfriend, Charley Stern, since ten o'clock. She never realized how slowly time could pass.

"Boyfriend? Try *husband,*" she muttered under her breath, testing the word out loud. She had to admit, the idea was starting to grow on her.

House with a pool, kids, school lunches . . .

It struck Casey how much life would change if she said just one little word: *Yes*.

A couple of weeks earlier, Charley had flown to Wilder University from California to propose to her. But instead of feeling romantic bliss, Casey felt emotionally ambushed. Of course, she loved him; she loved him to death. Her talented former costar on the hit TV show *The President's Daughter,* Charley was gorgeous, smart, funny, and sensitive, as well as a great actor. More than one teen magazine had named them one of the top ten cutest couples in America.

Casey *didn't* say yes, and she didn't say no. She said she needed to think—and talk—about it. After two weeks of hard thinking and countless long-distance calls, she and Charley decided they needed to discuss it face-to-face.

"Am I ready to be Casey *Stern?*" she muttered for what felt like the thousandth time.

She heard a small laugh behind her. "What about Stern-*Fontaine?*"

Casey whirled around. Nancy was back, barefoot, in jeans and a black T-shirt, drying the back of her head with a towel.

"What do you think?" Casey appealed to her.

Nancy's sky blue eyes sparkled with curiosity. "It's not what I think that's important. The question is, what do *you* think?"

"Marriage is such a huge step," Casey said, shaking her head. "And Charley's always been in a rush. The guy was a TV star when he was twelve!"

"And a sex symbol at seventeen," Nancy reminded her. "Life in the fast lane. Must be rough."

Casey blew a stray hair out of her eyes. "I'm just starting to find out what being a college student is like. Believe it or not, I'm really getting into Russian lit. Why couldn't he have waited three or four years?"

"Who died?" came the all-too-familiar voice of Stephanie Keats. Casey's roommate sauntered down the hall wearing a black spandex outfit that looked like exercise wear but on Stephanie would never even get sweaty.

"You two look so serious," Stephanie drawled.

Casey smiled to herself. Stephanie, the only woman alive who thought being a couch potato made her an athlete, hadn't exercised a day in her life. But she had a great body, long and lean, and was a believer in clothes of the skin-tight variety.

"She's waiting for Charley," Nancy explained.

"Really!" Stephanie said, feigning surprise. "It's getting to be a permanent condition."

Nancy sniffed. "What's that smell?"

Casey eyed Stephanie's outfit. "Why is it that every time Charley is about to arrive, you appear wearing next to nothing and smelling like a perfume factory?"

Stephanie tossed her head. "I have absolutely no idea what you're talking about."

There was a knock on the suite door. Stephanie smoothed her long dark hair.

As she reached for the knob, Casey's heart began to gallop. Seeing Charley always gave her a little jolt of excitement. *I still love him after all,* she thought, and twisted the knob.

The doorway filled with a lean, tall man with swept-back hair and a movie star's dark, piercing eyes. "Charley," Casey said as she exhaled the breath she'd been holding.

"Hi." He smiled, folding Casey into his arms.

"I'm so happy you're here." Casey snuggled deeper into him.

"So am I." Charley kissed the top of her head and stepped back to look around. "Hi, Nancy, Stephanie," he said.

Nancy gave Charley a mock stern look. "Hi, Charley. It's about time you got here. Casey's been counting the seconds since she got out of bed. Speaking of which—" Nancy looked at her watch. "I have to go! It's almost eleven, and I've got to meet Jake, George, and Will. See you guys later," she called over her shoulder as she left.

"So, Charley," Stephanie said. "How does it feel to be the future Mr. Fontaine?"

Casey took a step back. Charley was beaming down at her. "*Mr.* Fontaine," he said dreamily. "I kind of like the sound of that."

Stephanie sashayed across the lounge to drape herself over the couch. "But think of everything you'll be giving up," she said suggestively.

"I'm ready," Charley said sincerely.

But am I? Casey wondered.

Nancy was laughing as she walked toward the campus quad with her friend George Fayne, George's boyfriend, Will Blackfeather, and Nancy's boyfriend, Jake Collins. Nancy had just finished telling the story of Stephanie primed and ready for Charley in her skin-tight clothes and cloying perfume.

George shook her brown curls. "You have to hand it to her," she said. "She's amazingly resourceful."

Will shrugged. "So how come no boyfriend?"

5

Jake clapped Will on the shoulder. "Exactly," he answered, half joking. "But on to more important matters—"

Jake guided the group into the grassy expanse lined by stately classroom buildings on every side.

You're looking irresistibly gorgeous, Nancy thought, glancing at Jake in his jeans and cowboy boots, his light brown hair tousled as always.

She felt him grab her around the waist, and she collapsed against him a little, leaning her head against his familiar muscular shoulder.

Nancy and Jake had been dating since early in the semester. Their romance had started at the *Wilder Times,* where Jake, who was a junior at the university, was a senior reporter. Nancy, who had made cub reporter, occasionally collaborated on a story with him. Whether or not they were working, they always seemed to be together. And with each day that passed, Nancy's feelings for him grew stronger and stronger.

In the distance, she heard the noise of a large crowd. The far end of the quad was packed with people facing a small stage.

"Wow," George said. "There are a *lot* of people here."

Will nodded. "I didn't think there were that many people into animal rights."

"I bet that's what the university thought,

too," Jake commented. "They're in for a surprise."

It was Jake who'd told them about this demonstration to protest the abuses of research animals at a Wilder lab. He'd recently gotten involved with a campus animal rights group, which purportedly had discovered evidence that a research program at the Wilder Research Facility wasn't taking proper and humane care of the animals it was using for its experiments. There were even rumors of animals being put through painful tests for the sake of the research.

It was a crisp early-autumn day, and the air was electric with excitement. This was a serious demonstration, and many students felt deeply about animal abuse. A lot of people were carrying signs and posters with disturbing pictures of animals in cages. Students were handing out stacks of leaflets with addresses of animal rights groups in Washington. Everyone was fired up.

"It looks like a pep rally," George said, putting her arm around Will's waist.

"It sort of is," Jake replied. "We don't have to break down doors and scream to make a point, as long as the university administration can hear us. There are going to be lots of interesting speakers."

Nancy tugged on Jake's hand to pull him over a few steps so they'd have a better view.

"Have I told you that this is one of the things I like most about you?" she whispered. "That you care so much about ending animal abuse?"

"And do you care about it, too?"

Nancy searched his dark brown eyes. They were earnest, deep, full of emotion.

"Of course. Who wouldn't be concerned about the abuse of animals?" she replied.

"You'd be surprised," Jake said, pointing toward the stage.

Nancy looked up and noticed a man in a tweed jacket flanked by a few older graduate students.

"That's Professor Bailey," Jake explained. "He's in the bio department, and supposedly he's going to defend the university by describing what *really* goes on in the lab." Jake rolled his eyes. "He's nice, but he really doesn't get it."

Nancy felt a surge of excitement. "This is definitely what college is all about," she said. "Taking a stand on big issues."

Jake nodded toward the stage. "It looks like they're about to start. Let's get back to George and Will. This is going to be interesting."

Standing in front of her full-length mirror, Stephanie flashed herself an approving smile. Her long black hair had a slight wind-blown look. Stephanie's high cheekbones and feline eyes had been painstakingly made up to give her slim, sculpted face a special lift and that out-to-kill look.

"Drop-dead gorgeous," she thought out loud, holding a new peach-colored silk dress up to her neck.

More new clothes and credit card receipts were flung across her bed. The suite was quiet. Thank goodness, Casey and Charley, the two sticky lovebirds, had finally flown away, she thought. Most of the other women in the suite were at the animal rights protest. Stephanie's only interest in animals was the quality of their fur—for coats and hats.

Stephanie turned her head, exposing a long stretch of voluptuous neck. The dress wasn't much more than a fancy negligee. Perfect for a dinner date, Stephanie thought to herself.

"But with who?" she muttered despondently. She thought about how many guys she'd dated since she had come to Wilder, and realized she couldn't remember any of their names. They were all so boring.

"You're going to have to go out and get yourself an older man," she said to her reflection, zipping herself into a long black gown that exposed her lean, shapely back. Maybe one of the rich Wilder trustees.

"Daddy would have loved me in this dress," Stephanie mused. "Too bad now he wouldn't even notice."

There was a knock at the door. "Steph?" It was Kara Verbeck, Nancy's roommate.

"Not Miss Annoying," Stephanie muttered. "No one's here," she called out.

Kara laughed from behind the door. "Reva and I are going down to the cafeteria for brunch. Interested?"

"Let's see—rubberized French toast, puddles of eggs. Mmm-mm. Can't wait ... I don't think so."

After a pause Stephanie could hear Kara's footsteps fading down the hall.

Actually, she *was* kind of hungry. But Kara's syrupy sweetness and Reva Ross's hyperintelligent questions were the last things in the world—except maybe her new stepmother's playful little giggle—she wanted to deal with right now.

Wincing, Stephanie replayed in her mind her strained goodbye with her dad after his visit to Wilder. He'd brought along his new wife, Kiki. And, not surprisingly, Kiki turned out to be everything Stephanie had feared: irritatingly pretty, annoyingly peppy—and just ten years older than Stephanie.

Stephanie couldn't deny it: Kiki was a fast-forward version of herself. The only problem was, her father had eyes only for Kiki now.

"You didn't ask a single question about *me*, Dad," she complained to the mirror. "It was Kiki this, Kiki that. And thanks to her, it's goodbye Bahamas for Christmas. Now it's hiking out West." She mocked Kiki's energetic babble. "Nuts and berries, bears and soggy sleeping bags. Golly gee. What a plan. Thanks, geek."

Composing herself, she shimmied into a black leather miniskirt, the only thing she'd bothered to buy on sale. Usually, she wouldn't be caught dead buying sale items. But this one left nothing to the imagination. "Perfect," she commented.

But looking back at the thousand-dollar pile of debris on her bed, Stephanie felt anything *but* perfect. Not too long ago, her father would have bought all that for her. Now he saved his money for Kiki. Stephanie hadn't received a single present since she'd been at Wilder.

"But the Keatses aren't quitters," she reminded herself.

Her eyes fell hungrily on the credit cards stacked on her dresser with her makeup and hair accessories. She could still hear Kiki informing her that Mr. Keats was paying a lot for Stephanie to be at Wilder and that maybe Stephanie should lighten up on her spending. "Don't go wild," Kiki had said.

But staring at the little plastic cards, Stephanie felt as if they were the only connection to her father that she had left.

"Well," she said, "if that's the case, then it's your obligation as a dutiful, loving daughter to use them. Wild? She's clueless about what 'wild' really is!"

Bess Marvin dug deep into a big bag of potato chips and popped one into her mouth. "Here," she said between crunches, handing the bag to Paul Cody as they walked along the outskirts of Fraternity Row.

Paul, blue eyes glinting, wrapped a muscular arm around Bess's shoulder. Bess leaned into his embrace and smiled. All thoughts of the unread books and half-written notes they'd abandoned in their study carrels at the Rock, Wilder University's Rockhausen Library, evaporated from her mind.

"I guess our five-minute study break is over," she lamented.

"You mean our two-hour study break," Paul corrected her.

Bess shook her head. "Wow. Has it really been two hours?"

Paul nodded. "So much for your Western civ quiz tomorrow morning. And my chem lab."

Bess frowned. The fact was, Bess's schoolwork was on a roll since her disastrous first couple of weeks at Wilder. At the start of school, she was ready for the parties and dances and football games—all the really great stuff she'd been looking forward to since high school. She'd had so much trouble concentrating on classes that she'd been in danger of flunking out.

With the help of her friends, though, she got in a groove, lifting her grades higher and higher. Then, when she started dating Paul, she thought that having a sleek, athletic, doe-eyed upperclassman doting on her would help her confidence in the classroom even more.

But today's almost a total blow-off, she thought nervously.

Suddenly, a loud round of applause swept through the trees from the direction of the quad.

"What's going on?" Paul wondered, tugging Bess toward the quad's spiky iron gates.

"That big animal rights protest," Bess explained, gazing longingly through the gates. "I told Nancy and Jake I couldn't go because I had to study. I feel bad."

"Well, you *did* have to study," Paul said.

"Except that I didn't. Come on, let's take a look. It sounds exciting."

But Paul wrapped her in a full embrace. "I'm only interested in what's going on over here."

Bess peeled Paul's arms away, one after the other. "Come on," she pleaded, "it'll take only five minutes to take a peek and get back to the Rock."

"Yeah, right," Paul said, and laughed. "Just like it took five minutes to take a study break

13

to—how did you put it?—recharge our batteries?"

Bess looked at him. "Well? Aren't your batteries charged?"

Paul laughed. "*Overcharged* ... oh, by the way, how's life at Kappa these days?"

Bess eyed him. "Great, as always. And it's secretive. Which means I'm *not,* for the hundred-thousandth time, going to give away any of our sophisticated plans."

"Sophisticated plans?" Paul repeated. "So you guys *are* going to retaliate!"

Bess grinned and started to whistle, playing at being cool. Paul and his Zeta brothers had fired the first shot of what was turning out to be a little good-natured war against their sister sorority, the Kappas. One recent morning, the women had awakened to find the little sports car of Holly Thornton, Kappa vice president, on the porch of their Victorian sorority house. All the house could think about since was revenge.

Paul was laughing.

"What's so funny?" Bess asked.

"I was just thinking of the sound of your voice when you called that morning to see if Zeta was behind it all." Paul chuckled.

"Ha-ha," Bess deadpanned.

"I bet you guys are planning something good," he prodded.

Bess considered. Wouldn't you like to know, she thought, and shrugged.

"Come on, Bess, you can tell *me*," Paul cajoled.

Bess smiled—she liked to see Paul and his Zeta brothers sweat. All innocence and light, she asked, "What's to tell?"

CHAPTER 2

Wow." Nancy nodded at the student speaker up on the stage. "That was intense."

Jake folded his arms. "She's right. It is cruel to experiment on animals—especially for something as frivolous as testing cosmetics."

The crowd of demonstrators was murmuring. Over the last hour, students had come to the microphone to speak about animal abuse all over the world, and Nancy could hear people arguing about the speeches they'd heard.

Abruptly, Nancy became aware of a commotion to one side of the stage.

"I have a right to speak!" a girl was shouting as she pushed her way to the middle of the stage and tried to take the microphone.

"Let her talk!" someone shouted, and the crowd started chanting: "Let her talk!"

The girl grabbed the mike. Jake elbowed Nancy. "That's Amy," he whispered. "She's in my animal rescue group. She's also part of a more radical animal rights group. The ones who grabbed the dogs from the used-car lot and then trashed some of the owners' cars 'in protest.' "

Amy was tiny onstage. Waifish and pretty with long kinky hair, she was dressed in a flowing cotton skirt. "What we need to do," she pronounced in a high-pitched voice, "is storm the lab and rescue those animals. They're torturing them in there! Beautiful little kittens and puppies . . ."

There was a struggle for the mike. A tall man in a suit stepped up on the stage. "I'm Professor Bailey," he said, his mouth twisted in an embarrassed grin. "And I run the lab—"

Nancy wasn't surprised to hear some in the crowd start to boo and hiss. Professor Bailey waved his arms. "I understand your concerns," he said. "And I'm glad you're all interested. But let me assure you, no one's killing animals. And there are no kittens or puppies. I'd be happy to have any of you come down to the lab for a personal tour. But storming the lab will only be trouble."

Nancy turned as Will rested a hand on her

shoulder. "I don't know," he said skeptically. "He sounds convincing."

Nancy nodded. She thought so, too.

"Maybe, but what else was he going to say?" Jake retorted. " 'You're right, we *do* torture little kittens'?"

"Hey, there's Bill Graham." Nancy pointed toward the stage. Bill was a resident advisor on one of the men's floors in Nancy's dorm. He had joined the two older students flanking Professor Bailey, a man and a woman who were probably graduate students. "I didn't know Bill was involved in this thing."

"Isn't he a chem major?" George asked. "Maybe he works at the lab."

The woman next to Bill stepped forward and took the mike from Professor Bailey. Dressed in a white lab coat, she smiled down at the crowd. Next to Amy's jittery anger, she came across as calm and dependable. "You may not know this, but Wilder is involved with a number of important government and privately funded projects. Like one that's being funded by HealthTech Pharmaceutical."

Catcalls and whistles were tossed up onstage.

Staying composed, the woman smiled. "All right, all right, they may be a big, bad corporation," she said, her tone earnest, "but they're also committed to finding cures and treatments for diseases like Parkinson's and Alzheimer's.

And I doubt there's anyone here who doesn't believe in that."

She handed the mike to the other grad student. "Without animals," he continued, "there would be no research. Without research, no cure. And we are definitely *not* involved in any tests that hurt animals. Absolutely *no* animal is in pain or is suffering in our lab. Trust me. I have two dogs at home. I *love* animals."

Most of the crowd grew quiet. Professor Bailey came forward. "So the idea behind this demonstration is good," he said, "but it's unnecessary. I assure you that we treat our animals very well. Without those animal volunteers, our research goes nowhere."

"They're lying! I say let's storm the lab! Storm the lab!" Amy cried from the back of the stage. But this time, she didn't have as much support from the protesters. Only a handful continued chanting. In a few minutes, the demonstration quietly broke up.

Nancy, Jake, George, and Will moved off, a little less enthusiastically than before.

Jake shook his head. "I still think there must be something wrong going on in that lab."

"Well, they're not exactly going to admit it if there is," Nancy replied.

"You guys sound convinced to me," George jibed.

Will waved them off. "They're just reporters. Always trying to scare up a good story."

Nancy and Jake looked at each other and burst out laughing. "Yes, that's us," Nancy said, arching her eyebrows. "Always looking for trouble."

"I'm thirsty," George broke in, feigning a whining voice. "And hungry. And tired. And, and—"

"I see a double latte and a pile of gooey sticky buns," Nancy replied.

"All I can see is a pile of homework," Will lamented.

Nancy jeered playfully. "Later. You have all night. Now we're on a mission."

As they started to leave the demonstration and walk across campus toward Java Joe's, Jake lagged behind, glancing back toward the stage. The grass was littered with leaflets, signs, and soda cans. Amy and several other people were wandering around, filling up big trash bags.

"I think I should give them a hand," Jake said, stopping.

Nancy was surprised. *"You're* turning down coffee? The java king?"

Jake shrugged. "I want to help out. I'll catch up with you guys later."

Nancy, George, and Will watched him double back.

"Well, *he's* committed," George said admiringly.

Nancy nodded. She watched Jake, surprised.

She wondered just how committed he was. How far would he go for what he believed?

Shaking off her serious reverie, Nancy hooked elbows with George and Will and marched them across the quad. "Come on, I'm starving!"

Jake heard Nancy's laughter clear across the quad. Half of him wanted to follow that laugh, but the other half knew that he had other interests, and he had to give them at least some of his attention.

Sighing, Jake hitched a trash bag up on his shoulder and started picking up trash. Some of the others in the group were hanging out on the opposite side of the stage, but Jake had talked animal rights with them over and over during the last few weeks. He knew their arguments backward and forward. And, besides, he didn't mind a couple of minutes to himself.

The fact was, he felt confused about the protest. He knew that Professor Bailey wasn't telling the whole truth, but he wasn't actually lying either. He knew animal abuse happened all the time—but was it happening here at Wilder?

Jake heard whispered voices coming from somewhere behind the stage.

"This protest didn't get us anywhere."

"That professor dude washed everything out. It's time for something radical," a low voice argued urgently.

21

"Maybe we should go on another raid?"

"Definitely," another voice urged, "and to-night."

"Are you sure we'll be able to get in?"

"Don't worry about that. We'll find a way. We've picked locks before."

Jake froze. Was someone planning to break into the research lab? He had a pretty good hunch who it was.

A few minutes later, he spotted three people coming out from behind the stage, and knew he was right. He recognized them all. One was Amy, the girl who'd taken the stage during the demonstration. The two guys with her were named Mike and Chaz.

Mike and Chaz were part of the animal res-cue group that Jake and Amy belonged to, but, like Amy, they were also members of the radi-cal animal rights organization. Mike and Chaz had been involved with Amy in the stealing of the malnourished dogs from the used-car lot. And in the destruction of the car lot owner's property. Chaz, Mike, and Amy insisted on calling it an "involuntary liberation." It had been just another one of their so-called raids.

The three radicals slipped back behind the stage—to plan for tonight, Jake guessed.

The problem is, he thought, it's one thing to steal a few dogs, but it's another to break into a working lab. They were both crimes, he knew—but the second one had many more serious consequences. If they were caught breaking and entering, it could mean expulsion from Wilder—maybe even jail.

"Hey, you guys," he said, clearing his throat. He didn't know what he was going to say, but he was hoping he'd be able to talk them out of their scheme.

"I couldn't help overhearing—" he began, then stopped himself. The back of the stage was deserted. He circled the stage but couldn't find anybody.

They must have taken off. Those guys are about to cross a big line, into serious trouble, Jake thought. I don't want to have to turn them in to the police. But I have to do something to stop them.

"Mmmm, how about another?" Nancy asked, swallowing the last of her double latte.

George looked at her old friend and smiled. She had to laugh. She didn't remember Nancy ever working so hard to avoid schoolwork. They all had stuff due in class tomorrow, but it was too hard to spend a beautiful fall day in the library, especially after all the excitement. They had to decompress. And Java Joe's was the perfect place to do it.

"I want another coffee, too," Will said, sliding out of the booth. "George, how about you?"

George shook her head.

"Hang on," Nancy said as she rummaged around in the bottom of her book bag. "Let me give you some money. I know I have some change in here somewhere. . . ."

George cocked her head, listening to the sound of all the debris in Nancy's purse. "What happened to Miss Always Organized?" she asked.

"Left her at home when I went to college," Nancy commented distractedly.

Will waited a second, then smiled. "It's on me, Drew," he said, then walked off.

As Nancy began to close her bag, George caught a glimpse of the words "Journalism Assignment" across the top of a piece of paper. Nancy sometimes was tight-lipped about what she was working on, especially when she was on assignment for the *Wilder Times,* the campus newspaper. So George was curious. "What's that?" she asked.

Nancy shrugged. "Oh, nothing."

"You *never* tell me what you're working on anymore," George complained good-naturedly. "And as one of your oldest and best friends, I think I have a right to know."

Nancy looked at her. "Why?"

"Because you know I'll find out eventually, so you may as well get it over with now!"

Laughing, Nancy slid the paper across the table. "As long as you *must* know—it's an assignment I got on Friday," Nancy explained as

George scanned the page. "Everyone in Journalism 101 has to do a historical profile piece on someone who has lived in Weston for a long time."

George studied her and the paper skeptically. "Are there really enough interesting people in Weston to go around?" she asked. "Yawn."

"That's the problem," Nancy said. "Everyone else in class is writing about a retired political figure or a store owner or something. I—"

"You want to find someone completely different," George cut in. "Original. Do I know the way you think or what?"

Nancy threw George an injured look. "Am I that obvious?"

"Only occasionally." George laughed. "But you're right. You need someone really interesting."

Nancy pursed her lips. "Any bright ideas? I don't know if Weston has anyone like that."

"Hmm." George squinted. "Nothing yet. But here comes a guy who usually has a good idea or two . . . hey there, Will."

Clutching two large coffees, Will glanced suspiciously from George to Nancy and back to George. "What did I do now?"

George and Nancy burst out laughing together. "Nothing," George said.

"Yet," Nancy added, relieving Will of one of the coffees. Grabbing him by the hand, she pulled him down on to the space in the booth beside her. "But maybe you're about to save me."

Too bad Will wasn't any help, Nancy thought to herself as she crossed the quad, back toward Thayer Hall later that afternoon.

Racking her brains all the way to her dorm, Nancy still couldn't come up with a thing. "I have to get out more," she said to herself as she pushed through the door to her own suite. "See the world outside Wilder U."

"Nancy!"

Nancy was surprised to find Jake waiting for her. She'd been so deep in thought that she didn't see him sitting on the couch in the lounge.

"How'd you get in?" she asked.

But before Jake could answer, a second voice called from down the hall, "What do you think of this one?"

Quickly, Jake mouthed: "Help!"

Stephanie appeared in a tight yellow dress, her arms stretched wide. "Ta-dah! . . . Oh, Nancy."

"Hi, Steph," Nancy said gleefully. "I like the outfit. It's, um, quite—"

"Daring?" Jake suggested.

"I was going to say 'baring.' " Nancy threw Jake a knowing look. "Thanks for the fashion show, Steph," she said, grabbing his hand.

"So, you like it, Jake?" Stephanie asked as they passed her heading down the hall.

Jake turned his head, but Nancy gave his hand a tug toward her room. "Very classy, Steph," he said as Nancy yanked him inside.

"You're so gallant." Nancy laughed when she finally got her door closed.

Jake sat on Kara's bed and breathed a sigh of relief. "I thought you'd never get back."

"So how was the rally clean-up?" Nancy asked, a glint in her eye. "Ready to switch your major to sanitation engineering yet?"

Wincing, Jake reached for his lower back. "I have a sudden, great admiration for our garbage collectors."

Leaning back, he arranged the pillows behind his head. He and Nancy lay stretched out on top of the two twin beds, their heads turned to gaze at each other across the small space between them.

"What's wrong? You look worried," Nancy said.

"I am worried," he replied. "I overheard something I probably wasn't meant to hear, though I'm kind of glad I did. Amy and the two guys from the animal rights group, Chaz and Mike—"

"The dog thieves?" Nancy asked.

Jake nodded. "Yes, but I think they're about to graduate to something worse. Like breaking into the lab and freeing all the animals. Tonight. In fact"—he peered over at Nancy's watch—"as soon as it gets dark."

Nancy sat up. "And you told them that was a terrible idea, right?"

Jake shook his head. "Unfortunately, they took off before I could. They don't even know I overheard them."

"Jake, you can't let them do that!" Nancy insisted. "The university's going to know who did it. And what are they going to do with all those animals?"

Jake reached over for the phone. "Toss over your student directory." Nancy stood up and handed him the thick phone book. Jake looked up a number and dialed. He listened for a minute, hung up, looked up another number, and dialed again. Then he hung up. He stared blankly at the phone.

"Not in," Nancy surmised.

"We have to stop them before they do something they're going to regret."

Nancy sat on the edge of her windowsill and looked out. "So what do you want to do—after we get something to eat?"

"Get down to the lab before Amy and the guys do," Jake said.

Nancy started to answer, then hesitated. She wanted to help, but she wasn't sure she wanted to get involved.

"You don't want to come?" Jake asked.

Nancy could hear the disappointment in his

voice. "I don't know. Maybe it's a risk we shouldn't have to take. What happens if *we* get caught?"

Sighing, Jake sat beside Nancy. "I don't agree with how they get things done, but their hearts are in the right place. I don't want to sic the police on them. And we won't get caught."

Nancy thought a minute. It seemed a little dangerous. But in her mind, she imagined Jake and herself convincing those guys that there were better ways to make a difference. "Okay," she said. "Let's go."

"But it's nowhere near dark yet."

Nancy slid closer to Jake. "Good," she whispered suggestively. "Then we have time to prepare."

Jake threw her a quizzical look. "What do you mean?"

Nancy circled his neck with her arms. "Shh," she said softly, and, leaning in, she reached for Jake's mouth with her own.

CHAPTER 3

Montana Smith sauntered down the stairs of the Pi Phi sorority house. She'd just spent the last hour going through the closets of a few of her sorority sisters. Now it was time to get a look at herself in the huge full-length mirror that was propped up against the wall by the front door. She was pretty sure that the day's work had been worth the effort.

"Looks like I struck silver." Montana grinned, gazing at herself approvingly.

She had on an amazing new find—one of her sisters had just come back from home with a great black bouclé high-waisted jacket.

And it fit Montana perfectly. It looked very vogue paired with her friend Nikki's new black suede shoes and a funky black hat, which she'd squeezed down over her mane of blond hair.

Montana loved clothes and jewelry because dressing up was fun. The Pi Phi closets contained the pieces to a giant puzzle. And every day it was a new challenge to see what she could put together. This time, she had to admit she looked pretty cool in the jacket and hat. Now all she needed was a thick scarf, and she'd have an excellent outfit.

"I can't believe I'm going to fail psych now!" Kara Verbeck's voice rang out from the living room.

"Come on, Kara," Nikki Bennett replied calmly. "Don't start freaking."

Montana smiled to herself. She and her other Pi Phi sisters loved Kara; that's why they'd rushed her to join Pi Phi. But Kara did tend to be a little dramatic.

"It was just so mean the way Stephanie bailed on Tim and me for our paper," Kara was moaning. "Now what are we going to do?"

Listening to the two women, Montana suddenly perked up. She'd just remembered the last time she'd been in Kara's dorm room. Montana closed her eyes and summoned up a mental picture of Kara's closet. Yup, she thought. There'd been a really great scarf there.

"I can't use my family because *I'm* not from an 'American stepfamily,'" Kara continued.

"And, of course, Tim's suggestion is that we write about him."

"What's his family like?" Nikki asked curiously.

Montana chuckled at the sound of Nikki's question. Tim Downing was Kara's boyfriend. He was an Alpha Delt and was very cute.

"His family's just like mine," Kara complained. "Normal as apple pie. Dullsville, U.S.A. He just wants to be the subject of our report so he can use the fraternity as his stepfamily."

Nikki nodded. "But that would be anything but dull," she said. "Maybe you can fudge it. The American Stepfamily—Redefined."

Kara looked at her. "No . . . don't think so. But whatever," she said dramatically. "All I know now is that I'm so hungry I'm about to faint. Maybe dinner will give me some fresh ideas. Tim's on his way."

Poor Kara. Montana shook her head. Everything was always a mini-crisis with her. Either she was totally up and full of energy, or else she was complaining about having to do any work at all.

Actually, Montana could probably help her with her psych paper. She didn't mind lending a hand to a fellow Pi Phi. Especially if she could get a particular loan out of it—say, a long wool scarf.

"Hey there, you two." Montana smiled as

she walked into the living room. "Check it out," she said, turning around so they could get the full effect of her new outfit.

"Nice shoes." Nikki smirked. "In fact, I think I once had a pair like that."

"No," Kara corrected her, "you just *bought* a pair like that."

Montana laughed. "And you haven't even had a chance to wear them yet? I'm terrible, aren't I?"

"But they look good with that jacket," Nikki admitted.

"So, Kara, I have this idea," Montana said.

"Once-in-a-lifetime opportunity!" Nikki quipped. "Quick, get a pen and paper and write down what she says."

"Ha-ha," Montana deadpanned. "Actually, Kara, I was thinking you might want to write about me—I mean, me and my stepfamily."

"And what's so special about *your* family?" Nikki asked, hands on hips.

"Well," Montana began, "both my parents have been divorced and remarried, and my father has been remarried again, but I still keep in touch with my first stepmother—who's also remarried again and has a brand-new baby, who is sort of my kid step-stepsister once removed, I guess. Right? Well, something like that."

Kara and Nikki were speechless. Kara shook

her head. "Wow," she said. "You're not a family. You're a whole country!"

"And a pretty good topic for your paper, right?" Montana asked, a glint in her eye.

"Oh, my gosh, this is great, you're perfect. Is there anything else that makes your family unusual?" Kara asked eagerly.

"Mmm, well, the other cool thing about my family is we all have ESP," Montana joked.

Nikki waved her off. "Yeah, right."

"Watch this," Montana said, putting her fingers to her temples and fluttering her eyelashes. "I'm thinking. Let's see. Don't tell me . . . you're going out—with Tim, of course."

"You hardly need ESP for *that*," Nikki muttered.

"I feel he's pretty close," Montana continued, ignoring her friend. "And he's brought something for you. Hmm. Wait, I can almost see it." She wrinkled her brow. "He's bringing you flowers. How sweet. But better still, he picked them himself!"

"Oh, sure." Kara laughed.

Just then the doorbell rang. Montana put her own fingers to her brow. "Hmmm. I'm feeling it. I'm feeling it. That must be Tim now."

Kara jumped up and went out to open the door. A minute later, Tim Downing poked his head into the living room.

"Hey, ladies," he said, grinning mischievously. "What are two good-looking women like yourselves doing home alone?"

"It *is* Sunday night," Nikki reminded him.

"So, does that mean you're studying?" Tim asked incredulously.

Montana and Nikki burst out laughing.

Kara wandered into the room after Tim, a puzzled expression on her face. In her fist was a small bouquet of wildflowers.

"Uh, Nikki," Kara said, "I'm going to put these in something."

As Kara was leaving, she stared at Montana once more, a long questioning stare. Then she shook her head and shrugged.

Montana looked at Nikki, who was leaning against the couch. "Did that look mean what I think it meant?" she asked.

"And what exactly would that be?"

"I think maybe she believes me," Montana said thoughtfully, then broke into a mischievous grin. "This could be fun."

"In here," Jake said, pointing as he slid over to the edge of the passenger seat of Nancy's Mustang.

Wilder University's research laboratory loomed ahead as Nancy took a turn onto a drive near the edge of campus. The two-story building was dark. The metal double doors were closed. Nancy pulled into the empty parking lot in front and shut off the engine. They sat a second in the quiet, listening.

"I don't hear anything," she said. "Or see anything. It looks deserted. Maybe we should call campus security."

Squinting up at the lab, Jake shook his head. "Maybe they realized what a bad idea it was and changed their minds. But if they didn't, I want to try to keep it between us—if I can."

Nancy reached over and pressed Jake's hand with her own. "Well, *your* heart is in the right place, at least."

"And so are theirs," Jake added firmly. "Let's give them a chance. Come on."

As they got out of the car, Nancy stopped abruptly. Something was weird. She sniffed. "What's that?"

Jake stopped, too. A chill ran up Nancy's spine. Something *was* wrong.

"Smell that?" she asked.

"It smells like smoke."

"Smoke and something else," Nancy whispered. "But I can't make out what it is. It isn't like anything I've ever smelled before."

"It's probably being carried over here on the wind from town," Jake said as he started up the steps.

Nancy felt creepy. "Be careful, Jake," she called out.

Jake was already up the steps and out of earshot. Nancy could just make him out in the dim light reaching for the door. But before he could grab the handle, the quiet of the night was shattered by an earsplitting wail.

Nancy froze. What was that noise? It was so loud, it felt as if it were inside her head.

And that smell. It was getting stronger.

Of course, it's an alarm, Nancy realized. A fire alarm—and it was coming from the lab!

"Jake, don't go in!" she cried. But it was too late. Jake was already gone.

Ouch! Stephanie thought as she ran her hands over her hips. She'd just wriggled into a new tight, black dress. This one's going to be hot! she thought.

In the distance, she could hear the campus clock tower chime seven o'clock and the wail from fire trucks. They were always roaring around campus, answering false alarms. Usually at the frats.

Checking herself out in the mirror, Stephanie raked her fingers through her hair, then shook it out. "So?" she prodded herself, arching a perfect eyebrow. "There certainly isn't any point in letting this little gem sit in the closet when I can walk around campus and show it off. It may be late, but there's still the library halls to stalk—and those lonely young men sitting in the booths at Java Joe's."

Stephanie reached behind her to zip up her back, but she couldn't make it. Now she had to go out there and ask one of her pesky little suitemates to give her a hand.

Where's Casey when I really need her? she thought.

Her giant hoop earrings swinging, Stephanie sashayed out into a dark and quiet hallway. Not a soul was there, but a light was on in the lounge.

"Can you zip me up?" Stephanie asked as she barged in. She stopped, smiling, then offered her back to Charley Stern, who was sitting on the couch. "No one else seems to be around," she said, trying her best to sound shy. "Could you—you know?"

Stephanie couldn't keep down the grin as Charley rose from the couch and stepped toward her. As he grabbed the zipper, his fingers grazed the skin on her back. Automatically, Stephanie's eyes shut. "Ooh," she purred. "That's nice."

"It's just a zipper," Charley said matter-of-factly, tugging it upward.

But Stephanie knew men. And she knew the silky touch of her own skin. They attracted each other like opposite poles of a magnet. Stephanie stepped back and pressed up against Charley. "Maybe it's easier if you're closer?"

"Not really . . ." Charley began to say.

Footsteps approached outside the suite. A key scraped against the lock. Stephanie whirled around just as the doorknob was turning.

"Thanks, Charley!" she cooed, circling her arms around his neck. Rising on her toes, she touched her cheek to Charley's and breathed in his ear. "You're the best," she added.

Charley cleared his throat and stiffly held Stephanie at arm's length. "Hi, Case," he said quickly, flashing his perfect teeth in a strained smile. "I was just—"

"Zipping me up," Stephanie said, and threw out her arms.

In the corner of her eye, she could see Charley blushing crimson from the neck up as Casey narrowed her eyes. Stephanie shrugged. "Thanks, Casey, for lending me your, hmmm, what is he now? Your boyfriend? Fiancé?"

"Don't mention it," Casey said.

"Nancy!"

As Nancy bolted through the door to the lab, she heard Jake's call.

Inside, the walls and floor of the entrance glowed smoldering red in the smoky light of the Exit sign. She started to cough.

The bonging of the fire alarm was almost deafening.

"Jake!" she cried, then coughed harder. She started to choke. She could hear the distant sound of sirens outside. But where was Jake? Going against everything she'd ever learned in all those fire drills in school, she ran deeper inside.

Nancy turned the corner. There was a staircase ahead, and at the bottom was the dim outline of someone kneeling over a crumpled figure.

For a second she stopped breathing. Who was hurt? Was it Jake? "Jake!" she yelled, her heartbeat throbbing in her ears.

The kneeling figure turned his head.

"It's Mike! One of the guys I was telling you about." The voice was Jake's.

"I thought it was you," Nancy said, her hands trembling.

"Help me get him outside."

Coughing, her eyes stinging from the acrid smoke, Nancy grabbed Mike's arms, and Jake grabbed the legs. They half-dragged him back through the hall and out the door and gently laid him in the grass.

Outside, the air was cool and pure, and Nancy breathed it in greedily. "Is he conscious?" she asked between coughs.

"He's barely breathing." Jake wheezed. "There's blood all over his head."

"Let's roll him over on his back."

"Help me get his backpack off," Jake said, struggling to undo the straps.

The plastic buckle was stuck—or too complicated. Nancy snapped it in two, ripped the pack off Mike's back, and tossed it to Jake. "Throw that in my car so we won't lose it."

While Jake ran over to the car, Nancy put

her ear to Mike's chest. His heartbeat was slow and weak. She felt his face. It was cold, clammy. His pulse was feeble.

Coming back, Jake spat in the grass. "I can *taste* that smoke."

"Maybe he fell down the stairs," Nancy thought out loud.

"Those fumes would knock anybody out," Jake replied.

"Did you see anyone else in there?" Nancy asked.

Jake shook his head. "It was too smoky. But I didn't hear any of the animals crying or anything. Maybe Amy and Chaz took them. Oh, I hope they all got out."

Nancy gently slapped Mike's face, but he wasn't coming around. "Okay." Her instincts slipped into gear. All those hours in a CPR course in River Heights were about to pay off. "Look out," she said, gently pushing Jake away.

Expertly, she pinched Mike's nose, lifted his neck, tilted his head back, and started giving him mouth-to-mouth.

Nancy could see the emergency lights of the fire trucks scissoring through the trees. "Hurry," she said.

"Is he going to be okay?" Jake asked.

"I don't know. He must have breathed in a lot of smoke."

Jake shook his head. "And that wasn't just smoke."

Nancy looked up at him. She knew what he meant. He was talking about that smell. "I know," she said.

Sirens wailing, lights flashing, the fire trucks pulled up. Nancy could see only two of them, but she could hear more on the way. Campus security cars roared up the drive behind. Walkie-talkies squawking, dozens of firefighters fanned out around the building, carrying fire extinguishers and dragging hoses.

"What do we have here, miss?" one firefighter asked, squatting next to Nancy. He saw Mike's head in the proper mouth-to-mouth position and nodded at Nancy. "Okay, you've done a good job. Let us take over."

Nancy straightened up and took Jake's hand as two paramedics ran over with oxygen and began working on Mike. She glanced back over her shoulder. The downstairs windows glowed with orange flame. Thick fire hoses snaked into the building. With deafening crashes, firefighters knocked out windows with their axes.

The smoke billowed out into the night.

CHAPTER 4

Walking hand in hand with Charley along the bank of the river, Casey could still taste the incredible dinner they'd just finished at Marcel's, an expensive French restaurant that just opened on the outskirts of Weston. The view over the river, the plate-glass window reflecting back the dozens of lit candles, the sight of the Wilder University buildings clustered together—it had all been so beautiful!

And they'd dressed the part. Casey dug out her most elegant piece of clothing, a pale blue silk antique dress that accented her red hair and hugged her graceful curves. Charley, as usual, had his hair slicked back and was dressed to kill in a dark wool blazer over a silk shirt and designer tie. Casey had to admit that they did look like Hollywood movie stars, and everyone in the restaurant had stared at them all night.

Casey rested her head on Charley's wide shoulder as they strolled. "Thanks for a wonderful dinner," she whispered.

The truth was that though dinner had been delicious, and they both looked great, the evening was anything but wonderful. Charley, usually playful and funny, was quiet and somber. Casey wasn't much better. Charley had politely asked about her classes, and she had politely asked about his part in a new movie that was about to start shooting. They'd talked about everything and nothing at all. Now they were just silent.

"So," Casey said, breaking the silence like a pebble thrown into a glassy pond. "We haven't talked about the big question."

"You mean the big answer," Charley replied quickly. "I'm glad you finally brought it up."

"I didn't bring anything up," Casey said. "It's hanging over us like a cloud."

Charley let go of Casey's hand, and automatically, Casey stiffened for a fight. If there was a worst way to handle a marriage proposal, this had to be it. So much for romance!

Casey stopped and faced the river.

"What happens if you stay here at Wilder?" Charley asked. "Won't you want your own boyfriend *here?* Won't you be lonely with me back in L.A.?—that is, if we stay together."

"I thought you just asked me to marry you," Casey said. "Now you're talking about breaking up?"

"I'm talking about what happens if you're here and I'm in L.A.," Charley said simply. "That's not going to be hard?"

"You think I can't handle a long-distance relationship?" Casey asked. "That I need to have someone near me all the time? That I probably think a Friday night date with some stranger is more important than the guy I love, even if he's far away?"

"I didn't mean it like that," Charley said.

"It sounds to me like you're the one who doesn't want a long-distance relationship," Casey murmured. "Maybe you're the one who doesn't like being single. Is that why you want to marry me? Too much temptation back in Hollywood?"

"Of course not," Charley insisted.

"Then why bring this up?" Casey asked.

"Because you said no."

Casey was so frustrated she could scream. "Charley, I didn't say no. I said I needed to think about it."

"Which really means no," he interrupted. "I've seen all the movies."

Casey snatched Charley's hand. He tried to pull away, but she dug in and held tight.

"Ow," Charley said. "Let go."

"No!" Casey said firmly. "Listen to me. We may be actors, but this is not a movie. This is our *life*. That's why I want to be sure. Look at how many marriages break up in Hollywood."

Now Casey gently pressed Charley's hand between hers. Her voice softened. "I don't want to be like them, Charley. When I get married, it's going to be because it's the right time and the right place. And the right person. And it's going to be forever."

She could feel Charley work a finger free and wrap it around one of hers. "But aren't I the right person?"

Casey softened. "You always were, Charley."

"But isn't it the right time?"

Casey sighed. "That's what I'm trying to figure out."

Nancy and Jake were standing side by side, watching the ambulance race down the drive toward the road.

A firefighter walked up, his face blackened by smoke. "He'll be okay," he said confidently. "He inhaled a lot of that junk, and he's got a nasty concussion from that fall, but he's a strong kid."

"Thanks," Jake said.

The firefighter nodded at Nancy. "Good work there. You did a fine job on that boy. You probably saved his life."

Jake took Nancy's hand. She squeezed his, suddenly feeling as if she wanted to collapse from exhaustion and nervousness. She turned back to the building. The fire was under control. Firefighters were wandering around, checking for flare-ups.

For the first time, Nancy noticed the crowd in front of the lab, standing in the headlights of the fire trucks. Students had gathered when they saw the flames and the trucks. Nancy recognized a few of them from her classes, and some of them called out and asked what had happened, but she was too tired to talk, or even to remember their names.

"The animal cages were all empty by the time we got upstairs," Nancy overheard a firefighter say to his captain. "No one knows where they are. They're just gone."

Nancy led Jake off to the side, out of the lights. "Did you hear that?"

Jake nodded. "We'd better find Amy and Chaz."

"You think they took them?"

"Who else?" Jake replied tightly.

As they headed for Nancy's Mustang, Nancy heard footsteps behind them.

"Hold on there," a gruff voice ordered. A campus security officer stopped in front of them. "Aren't you the two who were here when the fire department pulled up?"

The tone of his voice was accusing, and Nancy wondered what was on his mind.

But why should I be worried? she decided. We didn't do anything wrong. She nodded to the officer. "That's us."

"The Weston police want to ask you a few questions."

Two police officers from the town of Weston walked over. "Is this them?" one of them asked. When the security officer nodded, the policeman turned to Jake and Nancy. "What were you two doing up here?"

"Nothing," Jake replied curtly.

"Really!" one of the officers said sarcastically.

"Are you implying we had something to do with the fire?" Nancy wanted to know.

"Don't *you* think it's a little suspicious that you were the only ones here besides that unconscious boy?" the officer asked.

Nancy narrowed her eyes. "That doesn't prove anything," she insisted, her voice rising defensively. "Look, we had nothing to do with that fire."

"Then just tell us what you were doing up here. And why were you leaving so quickly now?" the younger officer, who had a blond mustache, asked.

Nancy wanted to tell them about Amy and Chaz, but when Jake didn't say a word, she

48

kept silent. Say something, she said to him in her mind. Why don't you tell them?

"Do you two know this Mike character?" the older officer asked.

"I know him," Jake replied.

"And were you at the demonstration today?"

Nancy nodded. "We were, and so were several hundred other people."

"But several hundred people weren't up here when the fire started, young lady," the older man chastised her. "Only you two, and him. So add it up. Empty animal cages, an attempt to burn down the lab, three animal rights radicals caught outside—"

"We're not animal rights radicals!" Nancy shot back.

"Then tell us what you were doing up here," the man insisted.

Nancy knew Jake was keeping quiet because he wanted to find Amy and Chaz before incriminating them.

But he can't talk to them behind bars, she realized. She eyed Jake, trying to get his attention, but he was staring dead ahead. He looked furious.

"Well," the younger officer said, tapping his foot. "It looks like you two were in the wrong place at the wrong time. You'd better come with us."

Nancy hesitated. "Where?" she asked.

"Down to the station."

"The campus police station?" Jake wanted to know.

The officer cleared his throat. "I think this is a matter for the Weston police now."

"I can't believe this," Jake muttered as he and Nancy were led toward a squad car.

"I can," Nancy whispered tensely. "Wouldn't you be suspicious if you were them?"

Yes, Jake replied inwardly, but he wasn't going to admit it. He knew he was letting them be dragged deeper into this. He also knew he could clear the whole thing up just by reporting what he'd overheard after the demonstration that day.

"But we're safe," he told her under his breath. "They can't prove we had anything to do with it, and they can't hold us without physical evidence."

"But there's plenty of circumstantial evidence," Nancy fired back, her voice laced with irritation. "As the officer just said," Nancy reminded him, "wrong place at the wrong time."

Jake shook his head. "They can't touch us. I have to talk to Amy and Chaz before they do."

In the corner of his eye, he could see Nancy shaking her head. Trust me, he wanted to say.

But before he could, he was startled by a face in the crowd of students. It was Gail Gardeski, the editor-in-chief of the *Wilder Times*. She was concentrating on an officer's every word, scribbling notes in her reporter's notebook.

Gail raised her eyes and spotted Jake. Then she looked quizzically at Nancy—and at the police surrounding them. She cocked her head, her normally keen eyes full of confusion.

"Jake?" she called out. "I heard about the fire and called you to cover the story. But I guess"—she glanced back and forth between him and the police—"I guess you were already here."

Jake could feel his face heat up with humiliation. *He* was the *Times*'s star reporter. *He* should have been here covering the story, but he couldn't—because he and Nancy *were* the story!

"It's just some dumb misunderstanding," he said nonchalantly.

Gail looked at Nancy, her eyes hardening. "Is that true?"

But Jake could tell by the expression on Nancy's face that she was mortified. Jake knew Gail, and if she thought they were really mixed up in this—well, Gail had fired and demoted reporters for a lot less.

As the police nudged Jake and Nancy along, Gail's expression turned stony. She lifted her notepad and pen. "What's your connection to the fire?" she called out as if she didn't know them.

"Are you investigating us?" Jake asked her.

But Gail didn't answer. Just as the young officer opened the back door of the cruiser, she repeated her question, loudly enough for everyone to hear. In the corner of his eye, Jake saw Nancy wince. Ducking into the back of the squad car, he looked up at Gail helplessly and said apologetically, "No comment."

"Aren't you still hungry?" Kara asked, tossing the last bite-size candy bar into her mouth.

Tim leaned back in his chair and surveyed the pile of rubble before them. Candy wrappers and soda cans lay strewn across Kara's desk and the floor underneath their feet.

"You've got to be kidding." He laughed and nodded at the book in Kara's hands. "Learning anything useful?"

For the last two hours, they'd been sitting elbow to elbow at Kara's desk, Kara with her nose buried in a library book titled *ESP and the Paranormal Mind,* filling page after page in her notebook.

Tim, meanwhile, was becoming more and more exasperated. He was trying to work on the outline for their psych paper. Montana's family tree was incredibly complicated. It had so many branches that Tim was already spilling off onto other sheets of paper.

"It's amazing what people can do with their minds," Kara said with disbelief. "Like bend spoons and stuff."

Glancing down at the family tree, Tim scratched his forehead with his pencil. "Montana's family is totally insane. I bet they have to use name tags at holidays."

Kara shrugged and shook her book. "Whatever. I'm much more interested in *this*. I think we should test Montana. Listen, all we have to do is get some of those special psychology testing cards with the shapes and designs on them, and Montana will tell us what they are. I want to see if she can really do this. Maybe we can find those cards somewhere in the psych building."

"Kara—" Tim began, but Kara cut him off.

"Hey, isn't there a psych course in the catalog on paranormal stuff?" she asked excitedly.

Tim shook his head with disbelief. "I've never seen you so inspired to work," he said.

But Kara's mind was already speeding off in another direction. Her eyes scanned the littered desk as her stomach gave a plaintive rumble. She hopped to her feet. "I need more snacks," she announced.

Tim hid his eyes. "Not again."

Kara planted a kiss on Tim's cheek. "I'll be right back."

Halfway down the hall, Kara nearly ran into Stephanie who was carrying a couple of shopping bags. "Shopping again, Steph?" Kara asked, enviously eyeing the names of the stores on the sides of the bags.

Stephanie sighed. "No, none of the stores are open on Sunday night. I didn't have anything else to do, so I was just organizing my closet. Some of my stuff has to live in bags because the closets are so tiny here."

Kara grinned. "I'd be happy to help you out by storing some of your stuff if you need extra space. Especially any of your new stuff."

"I'm going to ask you one more time," said the detective seated across the table from Nancy and Jake. For just over an hour, they had been in a small room at the Weston police station, answering the same questions over and over. "Are you sure your statements contain *every* piece of information you have about this fire?"

Nancy squirmed a little under the man's withering stare. It was the fourth time he'd asked that question. He definitely thought that they knew more than they were saying.

What's the point of holding out? she wondered. We don't have anything to hide.

"I'm going to let you two think about that," he said, then left the room.

Nancy leaned toward Jake, who had been holding his hands so tightly that they were white at the knuckles.

"He's about to get mad, Jake," Nancy whispered. "It's too late to get to Amy and Chaz, anyway. If they're innocent, they'll be able to

clear themselves. And if they did have something to do with it, you have to let the police
know."

Nancy could see by the expression in Jake's
eyes that he'd reached the same conclusion but
just needed to be nudged. This was a serious
crime. The detectives had told them that there
was probably hundreds of thousands of dollars'
worth of damage. And Mike was badly hurt.
They were going to charge someone not only
with arson but also with assault and reckless
endangerment.

The detective returned and sat across from
them.

Jake took a big breath and said, "Okay."
Then he told the man everything he knew,
from what he overheard Chaz, Amy, and Mike
saying, to the names of a few other radical
members in the animal rescue group.

"Let me get this straight," the detective said
incredulously. "You're a part of this rescue
group yourself, and both of you were at that
demonstration, but you say that you didn't
have anything to do with the fire?"

Jake nodded. "That's right. Those guys *are*
part of the animal rescue group I'm in, but our
organization would never do anything illegal
like this. The animal rescue group is only interested in helping find homes for stray or abandoned animals."

Jake sighed. "You have to understand," he went on, "that there's another, more radical group of students who believe in taking action against anyone inflicting abuse on animals. Amy, Chaz, and Mike are part of this radical element. Whatever they did, they were on their own. No one else knew anything."

Tapping his pencil on his notepad, the detective looked grim and unsatisfied. "You're sure?"

Jake nodded, but Nancy had to admit that his confession didn't sound as good as she'd thought it would. After all, in the eyes of the police, they had all the reason in the world to finger someone else.

We're in deep, she realized suddenly. We need help.

"Can we go now?" Nancy asked, getting up from her chair.

The detective nodded. "But don't go far. I'm sure we'll be calling on you."

"We told you everything we know," Jake insisted.

The officer stared at them stonily. "Just don't leave campus without telling us where you're going. Wait in the hall outside. I'll have someone give you a lift back to your car."

Outside, Nancy headed straight for the pay phone. "Who are you calling?" Jake asked, trying to keep up.

"My father," Nancy said as she dropped a dollar's worth of change in the phone.

Carson Drew was one of the state's most renowned criminal attorneys. He was also Nancy's father, and when she heard his voice on the other end of the line, she sagged against the wall with relief. "Dad," she said, "are you sitting down?"

By the time she finished the story, she could practically hear her father's legal wheels churning in his brain. "Okay, now listen," he said. "It sounds to me like they don't have enough to arrest you. But if they want to question you further, call me right away. I can be there in two hours."

"Okay," Nancy said.

"But I do have one question," her father continued. "Why did you wait so long to tell them the truth? That's one of the reasons the police must suspect you."

"That's a very good question," Nancy sadly said to her father as she looked over at Jake.

Sitting side by side in the back of the squad car, heading back to the lab, Jake put his hand on top of Nancy's and squeezed. Normally, she would have returned the touch, but her hand didn't move. Her mind was clouded with a nagging problem: Jake had dragged them into something dangerous and avoidable. Worse, Nancy thought, I let myself be dragged into it.

Here I am in my first year at college, she

mused. I'm finally on my own—and it could all blow up in my face. Even if we're not charged with a crime, we might be expelled. As much as I hate to admit it, just being accused of setting that fire was enough to make me mad. Jake didn't think. *I* didn't think.

Suddenly, another horrible image flooded her brain—Gail Gardeski taking notes. Since the paper came out on Mondays, the story could just make tomorrow's edition. What would the headline read?

Jake had fallen asleep on her shoulder. He was breathing evenly, looking as irresistible as ever. She wanted to kiss him. She wanted to yell at him. She wanted to run away and be alone. What did she really want?

"For this to be over," she said gloomily under her breath. "To find whoever set that fire and get this over with."

CHAPTER 5

Nancy's alarm clock had just begun to blare in her ear when her eyes flew open. Bringing out a hand from under her warm covers, she waved in the direction of the shelf by her bed.

After a few misses, she hit the clock and slapped off the alarm, then she yanked her arm back under the covers.

"No way am I getting out of bed yet," she said groggily.

She hadn't gotten much sleep the night before. It had been late by the time she dropped Jake off at his apartment and drove herself back to the dorm.

Suddenly, the memory of the entire night came flooding back, and Nancy sat bolt upright. She threw back her covers, grabbed the

jeans she's tossed over her chair the night before, and tugged them on. She reached for her
sweatshirt, but when she brought it near her
face, she wrinkled her nose. It smelled like
smoke and something else—that chemical
smell that had overwhelmed Jake and her at
the lab fire.

"Yuck," Nancy moaned, tossing the
sweatshirt into the bottom of her closet.

"Yuck is right," Kara moaned.

The pile of blankets on her roommate's
bed moved.

"Sorry," Nancy said. "I woke you, Kara."

Kara poked her head out from under the
blankets. She surveyed Nancy's outfit and
raised her brow. "In a hurry?"

"Well," Nancy began, "I've got a really busy
day. I wanted to get a jump on it and grab this
morning's paper."

"Have an article in this week, do you?"
Kara teased.

"Something like that," Nancy sighed, pulling
on a sweater.

Hurrying downstairs to the cafeteria, Nancy
was praying that Gail hadn't managed to get
something into the paper.

In the dining hall, she made a beeline for
the piles of *Wilder Times* in the corner and
snatched up a copy. She snapped it open and,
leaning against the wall, scanned the front

page. Instantly, she felt something inside her drop.

Gail hadn't wasted any time after they'd seen her at the lab. She'd managed to re-arrange the whole front page to accommodate the late-breaking story.

"Research Lab Goes Up in Flames," the front headline screamed. "Animals Missing and Research Destroyed. Are the Culprits Activists or Terrorists?"

Her heart pounding, Nancy's eyes quickly moved down the article, looking for her name or Jake's. That's weird, she thought when she didn't see them. She reread the whole thing.

As usual, Nancy had to admire Gail's crisp, no-nonsense reporting style. She'd managed to talk to a lot of the people in charge. Finally, Nancy found herself staring at one paragraph in particular:

"At the moment, one Wilder student is being held in custody after suffering the effects of severe smoke inhalation. The student is expected to regain consciousness within hours. The *Wilder Times* has also learned that a number of other unidentified students are being questioned at this time."

Carefully, Nancy folded the paper in half. Then she sighed. She was lucky, and she knew it. Jake, too. Gail had no reason to hold back their names except as a personal favor.

Of course, this doesn't mean she doesn't believe we're suspects, Nancy thought. But at least she's giving us anonymity—for now.

The only question is, how long?

The cafeteria was starting to fill up with students. Nancy eyed the plates of waffles and pancakes coming out of the griddle room, but she didn't move. She wasn't hungry. Her mind was racing—she and Jake were still suspects. And even if they were never arrested, Nancy knew that the university still might accuse them of being part of the group that went to the lab. That would mean that she and Jake could be charged with breaking and entering, not to mention vandalism.

"Great choices," Nancy muttered acidly.

If only you'd said something right away! she wanted to yell. But Jake was nowhere to be seen, and Nancy realized she was getting angrier and angrier at the way he'd handled himself the night before.

George was dreaming as she sat slumped over in the back of the lecture room. She was startled awake when she sensed all the students around her stand up and gather up their books. Her professor was heading out the door with his briefcase.

"Class is over?" George asked groggily.

"Good morning," someone said, laughing at her. "Big test next week. Got the date?"

"Uh, sure," she muttered, and looked at her

watch. It was eight-fifty. She'd yanked herself out of her warm, comfy bed just to fall back to sleep in class. That's what you get for picking the earliest class ever, she scolded herself.

Clutching her books to her chest, George joined the steady flow of students out of the building and into the crisp fall morning. I need coffee, George told herself, but when she got to Java Joe's, there was a line snaking out the door. Second choice: back to bed, she decided with a shrug, and turned toward her dorm, Jamison Hall.

"Hey, George!"

George stopped. Another dream?

"George!"

George turned. Before her stood Leslie King, Bess's roommate. George braced herself. Leslie once had been one of the most unfriendly, up-tight, neat-freak study-holics on campus. No one could believe it when she was paired with Bess, because they were such opposites. As talkative and open as Bess was, Leslie was a human ice cube whose idea of a good time was studying organic chemistry on a Saturday night.

But miraculously, after Bess helped Leslie during a terrible time, they had started to become friends. In fact, not long ago, they'd even double-dated at Anthony's, a dressed-down funky restaurant. Bess went with Paul, and Leslie went with a guy she had just started dating, Nathan, a fellow biochem major. Bess had told George how amazed she was at Leslie's transformation. She actually looked sweet and pretty, and laughed, and even told funny jokes.

"Hey," Leslie replied sunnily. "So how's everything going?"

George cocked her head, her eyes narrowed with suspicion. She was still having trouble shaking off her old image of Leslie.

"I'm okay," George said. "Kind of tired, I guess. You know how it is."

To her surprise, the bottom half of Leslie's face opened into a wide smile. Her eyes wrinkled and glowed, and she let out a little noise that sounded suspiciously like laughter.

"Yes," Leslie said. "I've been studying so much, I can hardly see straight."

George nodded, astounded, and replied, "I know what you mean," even though she didn't.

"So, I see you and Will around together a lot," Leslie said. "You guys having fun?"

"Oh, sure," George answered, dying to know where Leslie's stab at social chit-chat was leading.

"I really like Will," Leslie said resolutely. "He's, well, handsome—and nice."

George was speechless. As far as she'd known, Leslie didn't even know Will existed.

"So what sort of things do you guys do together?" Leslie prodded.

George wished Bess could see this. "Well, Leslie, I'll tell you," George said, deciding to go with it. It was like a psych experiment, and she was interested to see how it would all turn out. "We go dancing sometimes. We listen to music sometimes. Sometimes we go on long walks together—"

Leslie was nodding eagerly. "Really? Like where? Where's a good place to go for a walk here on campus?"

"Well, it depends," George said. It dawned on her just then that she knew what was on Leslie's mind. "Are you walking alone—or with someone else?"

Leslie blushed, and her eyes glittered prettily. "I'm so transparent, I'm afraid," she said.

George smiled. "It's okay. I'm all ears." This was fun! Leslie was rather charming, being so embarrassed.

Just then Will appeared. When he saw Leslie, he threw a wary glance in George's direction.

"I'm glad you're here," George said to him. "Leslie was just about to give me some late-breaking news."

Leslie eyed Will with suspicion, as if she was debating whether to keep talking. But she surprised George when she said, "I'm going to sound kind of silly."

George pinched the back of Will's arm. "Of course you won't," she said. "Right, Will?"

Will cleared his throat. "Of course!"

"Well," Leslie began, "I kind of need an idea for a date."

"A date . . ." George began, but caught herself before she could ruin the moment. She'd heard about Leslie's date, but George just couldn't picture it.

"The thing is," Leslie went on quickly, "this guy and I have been out only once before."

"With Bess and Paul, right?" George said.

Leslie nodded, obviously relieved that she wouldn't have to explain it all over again. "And we're supposed to go out again Wednesday night," she said. "I told him it was my turn to pick something for us to do. But I don't want to do the same thing. I'd like it to be something really special."

George smiled at Leslie's vulnerability and realized, to her surprise, she was liking her more and more. "Well, you guys could go to a concert or to a dance club," she suggested.

"Great ideas!" Leslie blurted. "A dance club! I like that one."

George laughed. "That's the spirit."

"Thanks," Leslie gushed. "I'll let you know how it goes."

"Not at all," George replied. As Leslie turned and melted into the crowd, George stared after her in disbelief.

Will was shaking his head. "You look as if you've had a vision," he told her.

"I think I have."

* * *

Jake was sitting on the couch in his apartment, blankly staring at the TV screen, his cowboy boots kicked up on a coffee table. There was some pointless talk show on, something about mothers who enjoyed dressing like their daughters. Normally, Jake liked to zone out on this stuff. Sometimes he even studied with the TV on because he liked the background noise. But now the sound was off. And the bagel sitting beside him wasn't touched. Jake couldn't eat or listen or do his homework. Tapping his fingers on his knee, he stared at the door. "Where is he?" he said out loud.

Finally, he heard footsteps in the hall pause outside his door. Jake was on his feet before the knocking began.

"Hey, come in," he said anxiously as he opened the door.

Bob, another friend from the animal rescue group, was standing there in a blue nylon windbreaker, looking as worried as Jake. Jake remembered Bob from their meetings and knew he wasn't part of the more radical element.

"I got your message," Bob said quickly as he stepped in.

Jake led him over to the couch. "Did you go down to the police station?"

Bob nodded. "Sure did. And you were right. Amy and Chaz were already down there. In fact, they called in everyone from the group for questioning. But Amy and Chaz were in there the longest. And when they finally came out, they didn't look happy."

Jake swallowed hard. "Did they confess?"

Bob shook his head.

Jake shot forward. "You're kidding! They're really saying they didn't do it?"

Bob shrugged. "I didn't get the particulars. But I wanted you to know that I told the police what I knew about those guys, too," he said sadly. "About Amy, Chaz, and Mike going on all those liberation raids and stuff."

"It's not your fault," Jake consoled him. "When they were doing that stuff, they knew they had to accept the consequences."

"I just don't want to feel like I'm ratting on friends," Bob said.

Jake nodded. "I know. But if you didn't say anything, it would have gotten worse for you. What about Mike?"

"Mike's fine," Bob said. "I heard he was awake this morning."

Jake cleared his throat. I hope he told them Nancy and I had nothing to do with it, he thought to himself. "I'm sorry it came to this," he said. "I never approved of their raids."

Bob was nodding. "Yeah, they really got out of hand this time."

"You think they did it, don't you?" Jake asked hesitantly.

Bob shrugged. "You and I both know they were there. How else could it have happened?"

Good question, Jake thought to himself. But just because I can't think of the answer doesn't mean there isn't one. Chaz, Amy, and Mike made a mistake breaking into the lab, that's for sure. But arson's a whole different thing. Mike almost died! Could they really have done it?

Jake was determined to find out. Not only for their sakes, but for his and Nancy's.

Wincing at the loud music from the boom box behind the counter at Java Joe's, Bess pushed her way through a throng of kids to where she'd spotted Nancy, George, and Will at a booth in the back. She fell into the booth next to Will.

"Now that you're here," George began, "I want to know what you're feeding Leslie."

Bess laughed happily. "Why, what did she do now?"

George shook her head. "Brace yourself, but Leslie practically accosted me after my first class."

"And George was just barely awake," Will teased. "It was pretty merciless."

"She was talking about another date she's going on with that guy. She wanted some advice on what they could do that would be really special. She was actually kind of sweet."

"What can I say?" Bess shrugged. "People really do change."

"Well, this seems to be for the better," Will said.

"With Leslie," Bess replied, *"any* change is for the better."

Of all people, Bess should know. Not long ago she had helped Leslie when she went through a major life-changing crisis. Leslie had almost had an emotional breakdown about her classes, and then, to top it off, she'd been accused of murder. Nancy had helped to clear her and find the real killer.

During the trauma, Leslie had turned to Bess for help, and despite weeks and weeks of staring wars and cold silence, Bess opened her heart to Leslie. The result was that they were actually becoming friends.

"All I can say is that she was very unsure about what to do for a 'special' date." George laughed.

"Well, this is new territory for her. It's just a matter of boosting her self-esteem. Anyway," Bess said excitedly, "I have *much* better gossip to share with you." She looked around the table carefully and paused.

"Come on!" George cried.

"Well," Bess began, leaning forward conspiratorially, "we've decided to implement Nancy's genius idea of revenge on the Zetas."

"You're still obsessing over that porch-parking stunt?" George asked.

"Quit laughing," Bess told her. "It wasn't funny. Anyway, they thought it was such a joke that we couldn't get out our front door? Well, we're going to see how they feel about being trapped in their house. Nancy's idea is going to blow away that amateurish car trick."

A few days ago, Nancy had given Bess the idea of sealing up the entire frat house—the locks, the windows, everything.

"When are you going to do it?" George asked.

"Wednesday night," Bess replied. "I can't wait! And they deserve everything they get."

"Whew!" Will said, leaning back. "Remind me never to get on your bad side."

"They started it," Bess said.

"Well, it sounds like a lot of fun." George grinned. "At least for the Kappas. Don't you think so, Nan?"

The three of them turned to her.

"Hmm— What?" Nancy said, startled. "Oh, yeah, great. Sounds like fun."

"Whoa," George murmured. "Hold back that enthusiasm a little, will you?"

Bess cocked her head and looked at her friend closely. Nancy had been silent ever since she sat down. Obviously, she hadn't been following the conversation. Bess could see that something was bothering her.

"What's wrong with you today, Nancy?" Bess asked. "Having you here right now is like spending time with a satellite." Bess twirled her finger around the side of her head. "You are out of it."

"Sorry," Nancy replied, blushing. "I'm just thinking about the front-page article in the *Times* this morning."

"The one about the fire at the lab!" George cried. "I read that. Can you believe those nutty animal rights people did that? And right after the protest, too."

"Yeah," Will agreed. "What were they thinking? Whoever did it didn't plan that very well."

"And all the damage they did." George let out a low whistle. "When those suspects are proved guilty, that's going to be major trouble."

Nancy winced. "Well, that's why I'm a little distracted," she admitted. Then she sighed. "Jake and I are the suspects in the article."

There was a long, loud pause. Finally, Bess sputtered, "No way!" She looked at George and Will, whose mouths were almost hanging open.

"Nancy," Bess whispered urgently, "what on earth happened?"

"Great question," Nancy muttered. Then she sighed and quickly recounted the events of the night before.

"Well, I can see why you're not exactly happy with Mr. Collins," George said as soon as Nancy had finished.

"But you did go along with it," Will pointed out.

"I know I did," Nancy said. "I'm as mad at myself as I am at Jake. But now, because we didn't say anything right away, the police don't believe we're telling the whole truth."

Bess cringed. "Maybe you should do something about that," she suggested, "instead of sitting here gabbing with us."

Nancy nodded. "Good idea. Thanks for listening, you guys," she said, and pulled herself out of the booth.

"Good luck," Bess called out as she watched Nancy snake through the crowded coffee bar toward the door.

"Wow, and I thought keeping the Kappa revenge secret was a big deal," she said.

CHAPTER 6

Relief surged through Nancy as she pulled up in her Mustang to the Wilder research lab. There were some broken windows on the second floor, as well as smoke damage to the outside of the building. But in the daylight, most of the damage to the lab was unnoticeable. Obviously, maintenance men had been working around the clock to keep the building open.

Inside, though, there were signs of the fire. The hallway to the left of the entrance was barricaded, and at the end of the hall the stairs were blocked off with yellow police tape.

Suddenly, Nancy froze. An officer stepped out of the stairwell down the hall. Was he one of the men from the night before? Would he recognize her?

It wasn't such a great idea to be seen here—not while she and Jake were considered suspects.

Nancy melted back into the crowd. Ducking into the open doorway of an empty classroom, she paused to catch her breath. When she poked her head back out into the hall, she saw that two more police had joined the first.

When the police left through the front doors, Nancy, checking her watch, said a silent "thank you" for lunchtime. Maybe now she'd be able to get upstairs to the lab for a quick look.

As casually as she could, she sauntered back down the hallway, then stepped over the tape.

For an instant, she felt a chill and paused. The night before, when Nancy had rushed into the building looking for Jake, this was where she'd seen Mike's body, crumpled on the floor. Only she hadn't been sure that it *was* Mike . . .

"Jake," she whispered, again feeling a wave of relief wash over her. Jake *wasn't* hurt.

Nancy took the stairs two at a time. At the top of the stairs to the right was a long hallway with closed doors to what looked like offices and classrooms. To the left was the entrance to one of the labs, where the fire had broken out.

The big double doors were open. There were no more police around, but Nancy did see some people cleaning up near a wall full of empty cages.

Nancy gasped. There had been a lot of animals! She remembered what she'd overheard

75

the firefighter saying the night before about finding the cages completely empty.

If the animals had just been released, she thought to herself, some of them would have been found hiding under desks, roaming the halls, or lying unconscious from smoke inhalation.

She didn't remember seeing any animals being carried out.

No, Nancy thought, Amy and Chaz definitely got them out. But what kind of animals were they? At the rally, Amy had said they were kittens and dogs, but Professor Bailey insisted they were using monkeys, rabbits, and mice. Observing the different sizes of the cages, Nancy decided Bailey was right. Some of the cages were as big as the ones she'd seen in the monkey house at the zoo; others were too small even for kittens. They had to be for mice.

Quickly, Nancy counted the empty cages and decided that Amy and Chaz had taken at least two dozen animals.

But where, Nancy wondered, had they stashed them?

"Excuse me, can I help you?"

Nancy whirled around and found herself face-to-face with a pleasant-looking young man in an orange vest. He was wearing a blue hat with the insignia of the fire marshal's office.

"Oh, well . . ." Nancy paused, thinking

quickly. "Actually, I'm from the *Wilder Times,*" she said. At least *that's* the truth! she thought to herself. "I'm just doing a follow-up story on the arson investigation. That is, I assume there is one?"

"Well," the young man said, checking Nancy out from head to toe, "don't you need a notebook or something?"

"Of course," Nancy replied, pulling one from her bag.

The young man cleared his throat. "The fire marshal's office is checking into the possibility of arson," he said, as if the line was well rehearsed.

Nancy quickly scribbled in her notebook. "And you are?"

"The deputy fire marshal," the man replied.

Nancy noticed him glancing through a doorway to the room next to the lab. The door was labeled 106, and through it Nancy could see a small office. She quickly surveyed the room.

Even to her untrained eye, she could see how the fire had been started. A pile of papers must have been stacked on a desk, which was then shoved against the wall—the wall between the office and the lab. The desk, or rather what was left of it, was as black as tar. Nancy was pretty sure that was where the fire had been the hottest—and burned the longest.

"We're still working on how the fire started," the deputy was saying. "When the full report is made, it will state deliberate arson as the cause of fire."

"Deliberate," Nancy repeated.

"Listen, I have to get back to work," the young man said. "But can I ask you a question?"

"Sure," Nancy replied, hoping he wasn't going to ask for her name.

"Why did your paper send another reporter over?" he asked. "We told all this to the woman who came by this morning."

Nancy had to force the smile to remain on her face. "Really?" she asked calmly. "Was she a small, dark-haired woman?"

"That's right," he said. "And she talked to the fire marshal."

"Right," Nancy agreed. "That was our editor. For a story this big, she likes to send out a number of different people to make sure we don't miss anything. It's like fishing with a net. You know how that is."

"Oh," the deputy replied uncertainly. "I guess I understand."

"Well, thanks for your help," Nancy said quickly, willing her heart to stop pounding.

That was way too close! Nancy thought as the deputy went back into the lab.

For some reason, it hadn't occurred to her that she wouldn't be the only *Wilder Times* reporter on the scene. She'd have to be careful of that in the future.

Poking her head into the little side office,

she was still thinking of what the deputy had said about deliberate fire. Nancy had figured that if Chaz, Amy, and Mike *had* caused the fire, it must have been an accident—which was bad enough. But deliberate! Why would they want to burn the lab? Wasn't the point just to save the animals?

Jake had assured her that the radicals' hearts were in the right place, but as Nancy surveyed the charred office, she wondered. She remembered they had smashed the cars in the used-car lot when they'd "liberated" the owner's abused guard dogs.

Kidnapping animals was one thing, but deliberately setting fire to an expensive research laboratory—that was something else. All of a sudden, any sympathy Nancy had for the radicals evaporated.

"It's terrible, isn't it?" A soft voice came from over Nancy's shoulder. "Amazing what kind of damage three kids can cause."

Nancy turned. The woman standing in the hallway was familiar, and Nancy was sure she'd seen her before, but she couldn't remember where. She had her shoulder-length dark blond hair pulled back in a ponytail, and she looked about thirty. She was wearing a white smock with the research lab logo stitched on the pocket.

"Do you know what kind of work they were doing here?" Nancy asked.

"Yes," the woman replied. "A big project for a pharmaceutical firm called HealthTech. I'm sorry, my name is Jeanette. Jeanette Rigaud. I worked on this project."

Just then Nancy recognized the woman. She'd been at the rally on Sunday, the one who'd spoken out about what was going on in the lab.

"I'm Nancy Drew," Nancy replied. "With the *Wilder Times*."

"It's incredible, really," Jeanette Rigaud continued. "Years of research were burned up in there. Thankfully, we just finished the final report on our big project, and it was submitted days ago. So we may have lost our research, but our results have survived. And I guess that's the important thing." She sighed. "It's such a shame when politics can guide young people to the wrong ends."

"Do you think this had something to do with the protest?" Nancy asked.

"Well, it must have," the woman said. "It seems a little too coincidental, wouldn't you say? And I heard a rumor that the three suspects were part of a radical animal rights group or something." She shrugged. "I sympathize with their cause, really. But not at this kind of expense."

"I guess this'll stop the research here for a while," Nancy surmised.

"Definitely here at the university," Jeanette

Rigaud said. "But with our results, HealthTech will be able to keep the project going at their own laboratories."

So much at stake, Nancy thought as she looked back into the burned office. So many people's efforts, money, and time destroyed.

She shuddered. *And Jake and I are in the middle of it.*

Hunched over in his cubicle at the *Wilder Times* office, Jake stared at the phone. When he'd arrived there late that morning, a pile of paper was waiting for him on his desk. Usually, as the paper's crack reporter, Jake got all the plum stories and controversial leads. But this was a pile of filler blurbs, stuff the freshmen interns usually had to do. He'd tried to ask Gail about it, but when he knocked on her door, she called out that she was too busy to talk. She'd never been too busy to talk to Jake before.

Jake picked up the phone and hit the redial button. "Hey, Kara?" he said in a low voice. "Yes, it's me again.... Yes, I know it's the hundredth time I've called in the last hour, but I really need to talk to Nancy.... Okay, well, same message. Call me here pronto. Thanks—"

Before he put down the phone, he heard Gail's door open. Jake rose and followed Gail, who was headed toward the exit at a quick pace.

"Gail!" Jake cried.

Gail stopped and turned around.

"I wanted to thank you," Jake said.

"For what?" Gail asked, confused.

"For—" Jake began, but then realized that if Gail *had* done him and Nancy a favor by keeping their names out of the article, then she wouldn't want to draw attention to it. Then again, he knew she couldn't protect them forever.

"I want the arson story," Jake said quickly.

Gail eyed him. "You? You've got to be kidding."

"Look, Gail, no one has a better motive to get to the bottom of that arson story than I do."

Gail narrowed her eyes. "You should know better than to ask," she said. "There's a conflict of interest."

Jake felt his breath leave him in a single whoosh. He knew she was right. Suddenly, though, Gail's eyes shifted toward the doorway. Jake turned. Nancy was standing there, watching and listening to them—she didn't seem too happy.

"No, I'm sorry, Jake. Look, I have to go," Gail said hurriedly, and left.

Alone, Jake and Nancy gazed at each other warily.

"Mike's going to be okay," Jake said. "They're saying you really did save his life."

"I hope he tells the police *we* had nothing to do with it," Nancy replied.

Jake cringed inwardly. "Actually, he did. The police called me just before I left my apartment."

Nancy's eyes widened in surprise. "They called you? What did they want?"

"They said Mike told them we had nothing to do with the break-in. Just like we said."

"Okay," Nancy began, obviously wanting to hear if there was more.

"But," Jake continued, "they also told me that if we were involved, it would make sense that Mike would try to cover for us."

Nancy's mouth was set in a straight line. "So you're saying they don't believe him," she said.

"Well, it means they don't have any reason to believe him," Jake explained. "And he just wanted us to know we weren't off the hook yet."

"Great," Nancy replied. "And since I found out from the deputy fire marshal that they're designating it deliberate arson, we're in even more trouble than we thought."

"Deliberate arson?" Jake asked.

"I thought that if your friends did set that fire, it would at least have been an accident," Nancy said. "But there's no way that fire was an accident. I saw how it started with my own eyes. It was definitely set on purpose." Nancy's voice was rising with anger. "And now we're lumped together with those people!"

Jake blinked. He'd never seen Nancy so upset. He touched her hand, but she didn't move. "I spoke to a friend from the animal rescue group," he said. "He saw Amy and Chaz down at the station." Jake stepped closer to her so he could speak quietly. "Nancy, they swear they didn't set that fire. Amy told him that there was someone else in the building with them, but they didn't see who it was."

"Convenient," Nancy cut in.

"Amy said they were in the lab getting the animals when they smelled the smoke themselves," Jake went on. "Then the alarms went off, and they all freaked out."

"But not before they got the animals out," Nancy pointed out. "Just in time, I guess. Lucky them."

"Look, she said Mike was supposed to follow them," Jake said. "They waited, but he never came out, and when they heard the sirens, they panicked and split."

Nancy still looked skeptical. "And you believe that?"

"I'm not sure."

"Mike didn't come out of a burning building, and they left?" Nancy pointed out. "What kind of friends are they? And what have they done with the animals? I suppose they haven't admitted to the police they were even there."

Jake shrugged disconsolately.

"I don't see how you can still be defending them," Nancy said, shaking her head. "That's why we're mixed up in this whole thing. Jake, if only you'd called the police from the beginning—"

"Look, Nancy," Jake interrupted angrily, "I didn't exactly twist your arm to come along with me."

They stared at each other, eyes blazing.

Finally, Jake said, "We need to talk about this. But not here." He looked around the newsroom. Already people had drifted a little closer to hear what was going on.

"You're right," Nancy agreed curtly. "We do need to talk." She glanced at her watch. "Listen. I have my volunteer session for Helping Hands today. I have to go see Anna right now." She paused as if deciding something. "Do you want to come with me?" she asked, trying to manage a tiny smile.

Jake breathed a sigh of relief. Things between them were definitely tense, but at least Nancy wasn't shutting him out completely.

"All I want right now is to be wherever you are," Jake said. "Just wait until you get back to your room and find the seven hundred messages I left for you."

"Seven hundred?" Nancy said. "I can definitely wait."

Leslie didn't know what to say. She was standing in her slip in front of the mirror, one unhappy eye on herself, the other on the door in case Bess came in.

You only have two days to figure this out, she warned herself. Maybe this would look better, she thought as she lifted her hair onto the top of her head. "Or maybe I should just cut it short like Casey Fontaine," she wondered aloud, squinting to imagine herself with a short bob.

She let her hair drop. It was hopelessly straight and dull. "Clothes are the answer," she muttered, and eyed the mostly drab dresses piled high on her bed. "But those things all make me look like I'm going to the country club for dinner."

Leslie gazed gloomily into the mirror. "But I'm stuck with you," she muttered to herself. "Though, maybe, I can be a little bit of someone else . . ."

Carefully, slyly, Leslie slid her eyes across the room. As usual, Bess's side was a mess. Her closet door was thrown open, the clothes inside so jumbled it looked like a dryer in motion.

"She's such a slob, how does she always come up with such nice, fun things to wear?"

Leslie wondered aloud. "There's only one way to find out."

Taking a big breath, Leslie stepped across the imaginary border between their two sides of the room and headed straight for Bess's closet.

"Hey, maybe you can teach me to drive," Anna Pederson said from the backseat of Nancy's Mustang.

Nancy grinned in the rearview mirror at the tall, thin girl in the backseat. Anna had soft brown eyes that were older and wiser than a twelve-year-old's should be.

"Don't you have to be sixteen to get a learner's permit?" Nancy asked.

Anna shrugged. "Rules," she scoffed playfully, and grinned back.

"My older cousin let me drive down the street when I was twelve," Jake piped up from the passenger seat.

Nancy threw him a mock glare. "Thanks a lot," she said.

When Nancy had first met Anna, she didn't know what to expect. Most of the kids who got involved with Helping Hands were there because they didn't get the attention they needed from their families. Nancy knew that Anna's mother had died three years earlier, when Anna was nine, and that her father often didn't get home from his job until late.

But though she was a little shy at first, Anna had turned out to be friendly and funny beyond her years. By the end of their first meeting, Nancy really felt like she had a little sister.

"So thanks for taking us to where you hang out," Jake said, twisting around in the passenger seat. "I haven't been in an arcade in a couple of years. It's amazing how realistic some of those combat games are getting."

"No problem, it was fun," Anna replied with a shrug. She blew a wisp of long blond hair out of her eyes. "My friends told me they thought you were pretty cool."

Nancy winked at Jake. At first, she was nervous about bringing Jake along. After all, she and Anna were just getting to know each other. But Jake had been really great with her. He was easygoing and treated her like a real person. Nancy knew that Anna was enjoying the extra attention, especially from an older guy.

Unfortunately, this lighthearted moment couldn't make her forget the larger trouble she and Jake were in. But it was nice, just for a while, to pretend that there wasn't any tension between them.

Which is exactly what they were both doing—pretending. She could see it in Jake's eyes. Behind his smile, his gaze was worried. Nancy knew what was on his mind, but he was making an effort to have a good time for now, and she would, too.

"Oh, turn here!" Anna said, pointing over Nancy's shoulder as Nancy was about to drive past a fork in the road.

"Where are we going?" Nancy asked.

"I want to show you guys the mansion," Anna said.

"There's a mansion in Weston that I didn't know about?" Nancy asked.

"Sure, it's the mansion of the guy who built practically all of Weston," Anna explained.

Just then the Mustang came around a curve, and Nancy gasped.

"You weren't kidding," she whispered. She pulled the car over to the side of the road.

"It's cool, isn't it?" Anna asked, leaning her chin on the back of Nancy's seat. She gazed up at the beautiful building. "I'd love to live there one day."

Nancy took in the huge building in front of her. There was an enormous black iron gate with a crest at the top—a curly, ornate *V*. Behind the gate was an immense rolling lawn with a well-tended garden and rows of carefully trimmed hedges and shrubs. The house itself was incredible, with a huge stone porch and four enormous columns supporting the roof. There was even a turret on one end of the house.

"If that was my house, I'd set it up as a cool party place and keep it open all the time," Anna said. "His wife lives there alone now, she's kind of weird, and doesn't ever let anyone inside. She's very private."

"That's too bad," Nancy said. "What's her name?"

"You mean you don't know?" Jake asked. "I thought you were just playing along."

"It's Mrs. Vandenbrock," Anna said.

"The Vandenbrock Estate," Jake explained. "Wendell Vandenbrock was a member of one of the most prominent families in Weston. They helped establish this town. Wendell was heavily into local politics and development."

"Was into?" Nancy asked.

"He died a number of years ago," Jake explained. "I think at least ten, but I'm not sure."

"And just his widow lives in the house now?" Nancy said.

"Her and the servants," Jake answered.

"No one sees her," Anna interrupted. "She's got this huge house and a big stretchy car. I've seen it around. She never says hello to anyone."

"I guess Wendell Vandenbrock would qualify as a prominent Weston citizen, right?" Nancy asked, thinking of her journalism profile.

"Sure," Jake replied.

"But he's not very interesting since he's no longer around," Anna pointed out dryly.

"But maybe *Mrs.* Vandenbrock can qualify

as a prominent citizen," Nancy mumbled. "And a wealthy recluse has a nice element of intrigue to it, don't you think?" Nancy turned to Jake. "That could be a way to make my journalism profile really different."

"What journalism profile?" Jake asked curiously.

"Yeah, what profile?" Anna chimed in.

"The one I'm going to write on Mrs. Vandenbrock," Nancy explained excitedly.

CHAPTER 7

It was Tuesday morning, and Stephanie was sitting on the edge of her bed, shuffling her credit cards. Her morning classes had been a total snore. All she could think of was getting out of class and going downtown to buy a pair of leather boots she'd spotted on a shopping trip the day before.

Stephanie sauntered out to the lounge to see which of her suitemates might be available to hang with.

"What luck," Stephanie drawled when she saw who was sitting on the couch. "Just the person I wanted to see."

Eileen O'Connor lifted her freckled face and stared at Stephanie.

"Me?" Eileen said, "What did I do?"

"Nothing, Eileen, I'm just"—Stephanie forced a smile—"really glad to see you. I have to run a few errands downtown, and I thought some company would be fun."

"Company?" Eileen frowned and wrinkled her brow suspiciously. "You want *my* company?" She narrowed her eyes. "For what?"

"Just a shopping trip," Stephanie replied. "A few stops here and there."

"Oh, I see," Eileen said. "You want to go shopping. Sorry, I can't." Eileen motioned to the books on the coffee table in front of her. "I've got tons to do, and anyway, I don't have any money."

"Oh, come on," Stephanie pleaded. "We won't spend any money, just go window shopping. I promise. I've just got to get out today. It's getting colder outside, and pretty soon we'll be stuck inside all day," Stephanie added. "Just think of it."

Raising her arms in mock surrender, Eileen burst out laughing. "Okay, okay, I give up," she said. "I don't know why you've chosen me, but fine. I *could* stand to get out. Only on one condition."

"Anything, of course," Stephanie replied sweetly.

"That, one, we're not actually buying," Eileen insisted. "And, two, I'm not going with you to carry your bags."

"Of course not." Stephanie grinned wickedly. "Just an innocent little stroll along the boulevard."

Nancy tossed her book bag onto the floor by her desk and dropped into her chair. She'd just come back from her journalism class. Her professor had given them more guidelines for their profile assignment.

Nancy already had a few ideas, and she wanted to get them down before she forgot them. She fished her notebook out from her bag and flipped on her computer. Waiting for the machine to boot up, she patted it on the top. How did I ever get along without you? she wondered, remembering the day her father brought her the computer as a gift.

Reva Ross, her computer expert suitemate, had helped Nancy set up everything, including installing her modem and getting her connected to the Internet so she could have her own E-mail address.

As soon as Nancy's computer screen blinked on, she saw that there was a little message light in the corner, signaling she had E-mail. Curious, she called it up. It was from her father, an article, snipped from a big Chicago newspaper: "Some Paper Goes Up in Smoke, But Hope Still Burns Brightly for Parkinson's Sufferers."

"Oh, no!" Nancy whispered as she quickly scanned her screen.

"A research lab at nearby Wilder University

was vandalized last night in an incident some are calling a blow for animal rights groups. . . ."

Her father had written a little note: "You've made the paper here, too!"

Unfortunately, Nancy didn't think it was very funny. The story had been reported in a national paper! There was no way her name and Jake's would be kept out of the news much longer. Not if they were still being investigated.

Nancy was about to stop reading when something caught her eye: "HealthTech Pharmaceutical." Carefully, she read the rest of the article.

The piece explained that although there were numerous research projects and studies going on in the Wilder lab, the only actual research destroyed was from a project for HealthTech.

Though a lot of raw data was lost, Health-Tech still had some very exciting results from the research that had been carried out, and the company had decided to go ahead with the announcement of a new drug it would be developing. Although the development of the drug was projected to cost millions of dollars, it could mean millions more in revenue for HealthTech.

Nancy couldn't help thinking how strange it was that the HealthTech project was the only "victim" in the lab fire. She'd first heard about the company at the demonstration.

Nancy drummed her fingers on her computer monitor. There's something important about the connection between HealthTech and the fire in the lab, she thought. Did Amy, Chaz, and Mike target HealthTech just because the project was mentioned at the demonstration? And if they did, how did they know where that research would be kept?

The door opened and slammed shut as Kara breezed into the room.

"Oh, Nancy!" she cried triumphantly. "I was just thinking of you, and look—here you are!"

"Well, this *is* my room," Nancy pointed out.

"True." Kara nodded solemnly. "I guess the probability for that was above average."

Nancy cocked her head. "Kara, what are you talking about?"

"Oh, nothing. Just a little project I'm working on," Kara replied. "Anyway, listen, I've got to tell you something serious—the cops were here this morning while you were in class."

"What?" Nancy cried. "What did they want?"

"Well," Kara explained, "there weren't many of us here. Just me and Reva and Eileen, I think. They just asked what we'd been doing Sunday night and if any of us knew where you were. I'm sorry I couldn't cover for you." Kara looked at Nancy curiously. "I mean, I was here in the room, and you weren't. Is this major trouble?"

Nancy dropped her head into her hands. Major trouble? she thought. National news, property damage, cops coming to her dorm? If there was any question about whether Nancy was really under investigation, Kara had just answered it. She was.

"I hope not," Nancy said.

"Do you want to talk about it?" Kara asked. "Is there anything I can do to help?"

"Actually, yes," Nancy replied. "You can help. The thing is, not only do I *not* want to talk about it, I want to stop thinking about it, too."

"Oh, so you want some distraction?" Kara grinned mischievously. "Well, that, I'm sure, I can help you with."

"No doubt." Nancy smiled.

"Okay, so listen to this project I'm working on," Kara began. "Montana Smith may have ESP! She says her whole family has this ability, and they communicate all the time. . . ."

Nancy tried to follow what Kara was telling her, even though it all sounded a little unbelievable. But all Nancy had to do was nod at the appropriate times and throw in a few affirmative comments. Kara pretty much kept up the conversation all by herself, and Nancy managed to be distracted for a full half hour.

Then Kara left to meet her boyfriend, Tim Downing.

Unfortunately, as soon as Kara left, the fire at the lab—and her future at Wilder—flooded back into Nancy's mind.

But I'd better make sure to take care of what's going on in the rest of my life, she warned herself. If I do get to stay in school, I'll need to hand in my assignment for journalism class.

Nancy sighed. Get back to work, she commanded herself. Stop dwelling on that fire.

Nancy flipped open her notebook and began transferring notes onto the computer. She also typed in a few of the story angle ideas she had about Mrs. Vandenbrock: "The widow of Weston; Weston's mysterious mansion and its elusive owner; Mrs. Vandenbrock—the woman behind the name."

Then Nancy went to the lounge, grabbed the local phone book, and took it back to her room. It wasn't hard to find the right number—there was only one Vandenbrock listed in the book.

She picked up the phone and punched in the number.

"Vandenbrock residence," a gruff male voice answered.

"Hello?" Nancy replied uncertainly. "I'm looking for Mrs. Vandenbrock, please."

"Who's calling?" the voice asked.

"My name is Nancy Drew. I'm a student at the university—"

"We give through regular channels, thank you," the voice replied, about to hang up.

"No, wait!" Nancy cried. "I don't want money. I'm a journalism major. I have an assignment to profile a prominent Weston resident."

"Yes?"

"And I hoped Mrs. Vandenbrock would give me an interview," Nancy finished, holding her breath.

There was silence on the other end.

"Hello?" Nancy asked again.

"Give me your name and number. I'll relay your message to Mrs. Vandenbrock," the gruff voice ordered. "If you don't hear from us, please don't call again."

Stunned, Nancy gave the man the information. The next second she heard a dial tone. "Wow," she murmured. "Mrs. Vandenbrock really doesn't like to be bothered."

Jake was about to take out his wallet and pay for his sandwich at the Underground when he found his mind drifting off. He saw himself at the lab again, smelling that weird chemical smoke. Then the police station flashed before him. "Tell them, Jake," he heard Nancy say again and again....

"Hey, buddy," the cashier said. "That'll be

four-fifty. Are you buying those apples, too? Then it's five even.''

Jake blinked. The Underground came back into focus. By day a dark basement café, at night it became the hottest hangout on campus, where bands played far into the night. But now the lights strung around the walls were off, and the sunlight streaming in through the windows wasn't enough to clear away his gloom.

The cashier cleared his throat. "Hello?''

"Sorry," Jake said as he paid and quickly went outside. He reached up to the back of his neck. His whole body was stiff with tension.

"I've got to let off some steam," he said to himself.

He slung his book bag over his shoulder and crossed the quad. Clumps of students were sitting on the grass eating lunch, reading, or napping.

Halfway down Waterman Street, in sight of his apartment house, he glimpsed one of his roommates, Nick Dimartini, turning the corner.

"Hey!" Jake called, and jogged up to catch him.

"How's it going, jailbird?" Nick joked.

But Jake wasn't laughing. He looked at his roommate. Nick wasn't tall, and he wasn't particularly athletic-looking, but he was the meanest pickup basketball player this side of the field house.

It's been a long time since we've hung out, Jake thought to himself. Nick is always so funny; no one can make me laugh like he does.

But after he'd met Nancy, Jake had spent all his time either with her or at the paper.

Maybe it's time I unearthed some of my old life, he mused. "What are you doing right now?" he asked.

Nick eyed him. "Why, what's up?"

"How about some severely mindless activity?" Jake suggested. "Hoops. At the field house. Twenty minutes."

Nick smiled broadly. "Great idea! You just saved me from an afternoon in the Rock."

Jake shrugged. "What are friends for if not to get you in trouble, blow off homework . . ."

CHAPTER 8

You have no one to blame but yourself, Eileen repeated over and over as she paused to readjust her hold on the seven shopping bags she was clutching.

"This is the last place, I promise," Stephanie said, breezing ahead of Eileen into yet another boutique.

"Yeah, right," Eileen muttered. "Like your other promises—*no* actual shopping, *no* spending real money, and definitely, absolutely, *no* bag carrying."

Eileen followed Stephanie into the boutique and immediately headed for the back, where a wall of mirrors reflected her tired and frustrated expression.

"I look like a pack horse," Eileen said, shaking her head at herself in the mirror.

She collapsed into a chair. By now she knew the routine. Stephanie would scour the boutique, grabbing hangers from the racks like a tornado blowing through the store. Then she'd take about a million things into the dressing room, complain about at least half of them, and buy half of what was left.

Eileen let her head fall back against the wall. What I really should be doing is studying, she thought wearily. I can't believe I let her talk me into this.

Eileen glanced around at the pricey fashions on the nearby mannequins. Suddenly, she found herself gazing at a satiny pink dress with a velvet bodice. Eileen could almost imagine how amazing it would look.

"On someone else, that is," she said.

No, Eileen suddenly thought. Wait a minute. Why on someone else? Eileen dumped all of Stephanie's bags onto the floor. No way am I coming out of this afternoon without doing anything fun, she decided.

Eileen grabbed the dress off the hanger and slipped into the dressing room. She pulled off her sweater and nervously unzipped the delicate, shimmery fabric. Carefully, she slipped the dress over her head. It felt like someone had just poured cool milk over her back.

Eileen couldn't wait to see it on. She reached for the handle and then paused.

"Okay, O'Connor," she muttered to herself. "Don't get your hopes up. The dress is going to be beautiful, but it's not going to turn you into a goddess or anything. So don't be disappointed."

Eileen flung open the dressing-room door. And gasped.

"Oh, there you are!" Stephanie cried, spotting Eileen in the mirror. "I was looking all over for you— Hey—" Stephanie paused and walked over to her. "That looks great!" she said, sounding as surprised as Eileen felt.

This time Eileen hardly recognized herself in the mirror. The soft pink of the velvet brought a blush to her cheeks and made her usually uninspired hair color practically glow.

"Yeah," Eileen said. "Only it probably costs about a hundred bucks. I knew I shouldn't have come shopping with you." Eileen shook her head. "I can't afford it, but now that I have it on, I don't think it's physically possible for me to take it off."

Stephanie laughed ruefully. Then she looked at Eileen and pursed her lips, deep in thought.

"Let me see," she said, grabbing the tag. "Well, you're not far off," she said, flicking the tag back into the armhole of the dress. "Okay, quick, take it off and give it to me."

"Gee, thanks, Steph," Eileen muttered.

"Rub it in, why don't you? I can't afford it, and you're going to buy it?"

"No, idiot," Stephanie muttered. "I'm going to buy it for *you*."

Eileen stared at her, openmouthed. "Are you kidding?"

"Look," Stephanie said. "My objective today is to spend money. Got it? Now, I'm also, for some reason I can't understand, feeling generous at this very moment. So take advantage of it," Stephanie argued, "or leave here dreaming wistfully about the you who could have been."

Eileen stared at her. "You *are* serious."

"Only for about another three minutes," Stephanie said, motioning Eileen to get the dress off and hand it over. "You'd better hurry."

Eileen ducked back into the dressing room and changed. When she came out, Stephanie snatched the dress from her.

"Just don't *ever* remind me that I did this," Stephanie said. But Eileen thought she detected the glimmer of a smile on her suitemate's face.

"Don't look a gift horse in the mouth," Eileen offered with a grin, suddenly remembering an upcoming Kappa formal party. This dress would be perfect.

"That's good advice," Stephanie muttered as she put the dress on top of a pile of clothes at the counter. "But don't call me a horse."

*   *   *

"Can I help you?" the woman behind the desk asked when Nancy entered the biochemistry graduate office. After reading the article her father had faxed her, Nancy wanted to get some more information on the HealthTech project. She figured the best way would be to go right to the source.

"Yes," Nancy replied pleasantly. "I was wondering if I could get some information on the grants the university receives for its research lab. I'm particularly interested in the private grants."

"Any particular one?"

"Well . . ." Nancy thought quickly. "This is for a friend who's a chemistry graduate and is thinking of applying to Wilder. He asked me to see what the research lab was doing."

"In that case," the secretary said, glancing around, "I can get you a list of projects from the computer."

Nancy waited while the woman printed out the information. Then she handed Nancy a few pages.

"You can just send this to him," she said. "He can see who donates the money and what the project is for."

Nancy glanced at the list. There was Health-Tech, right at the top.

"Oh, this looks great," Nancy said, pointing to the HealthTech name. "I know he's very interested in pharmaceutical work."

Nancy could see that HealthTech had been giving more than $200,000 a year for the past six years to the research lab for the development of a Parkinson's treatment.

"Professor Bailey is in charge of that program," the secretary explained. "You can talk to him, or you can have your friend speak to his graduate aide. Her name is Jeanette Rigaud." The secretary checked a list on her desk. "She's in room one-oh-six in the research lab."

"One-oh-six?" Nancy repeated. That was the office where the fire had started! How weird that when we spoke, Jeanette Rigaud never mentioned that it was her own office that was burned, Nancy thought.

"Well, thanks for the help." Nancy smiled distractedly. "I know my friend will appreciate the information."

Nancy left the building shaking her head. Okay, so Jeanette Rigaud had been upset about the fire, Nancy mused. But she'd also seemed very sympathetic to the protesters. In fact, Nancy recalled, she had thought it was a shame that a few kids could be misguided enough to cause so much damage.

Wait a minute! Nancy stopped in her tracks, the printout pages fluttering in her hands.

That's *not* what Jeanette Rigaud said, Nancy remembered. She'd said, what a shame that *three* kids could cause so much damage.

107

"Three kids," Nancy repeated, stunned.

On Monday, when Nancy spoke to Jeanette Rigaud, there was only *one* person in custody, and that was Mike. In the newspaper accounts, Gail had gone out of her way to mention "a number of suspects."

Nancy and Jake knew only three people were suspected of breaking into the lab. But they knew because Jake had heard Amy, Mike, and Chaz plan it. So how did Jeanette Rigaud know? Either she knew beforehand, or else she had seen them. Which she couldn't have done, unless she had been there!

Was it possible she was at the lab that night? Nancy wondered, then suddenly remembered what Jake had said about Amy and Chaz. Amy had told a friend of theirs that someone else was in the lab with them that night. Could that someone have been Jeanette Rigaud? And if so, why didn't Amy tell the police?

"Hey, isn't that—" Charley heard someone say behind him.

Charley tugged the brim of his baseball cap down lower on his face. Great disguise, Charley chided himself. I guess the old hat-and-sunglasses routine isn't enough to disguise me anymore.

If Casey was with him, he wouldn't expect to go unnoticed. As a couple, they really stuck out, especially with Casey's flame-red hair.

Charley sighed. But Casey was in class or in
the library or someplace. Wherever Casey was,
she wasn't with him.

Quickly crossing the quad, Charley felt in
his pocket for the key to his motel room. Of
course, he always felt like a stranger when he
came, especially since he had to stay in a
motel. But at least the Collegetown Motel was
getting used to him. He didn't even have to
sign autographs for them anymore. But even if
they were used to him, not everyone else on
campus was. He'd already signed ten autographs that day.

How does Casey deal with it? he wondered.
Then again, how would *I* deal with it, coming
up here to visit? Maybe it would get to the
point where people expected to see me. If Casey
is going to stay at Wilder—

If, he thought. If, if, if . . .

But I don't want her to stay.

Passing a trash can, he fired off the wrapper
of a candy bar he'd been eating and banked
it in.

That's what I want to do, he thought. Play
some ball. I have all this time to kill since
Casey's banished me from her dorm until six.

Charley knew his way to the field house.
Luckily, he was wearing high tops.

Pushing through the big doors, he was surprised to see only one game of hoops on the
floor. The shouts and dribbling of the ball

echoed through the cavernous room. Charley wandered over and was happy to see one of the guys was Jake Collins, Nancy Drew's boyfriend, someone he actually had gotten to know a bit.

"What's up, Jake?" Charley asked.

Jake raised his head, panting and dripping sweat. "Charley! Looking for a fight? Nick's on fire."

Charley grinned. "You read my mind."

"Nick, Charley Stern." Jake introduced them. "So when's the wedding day?" he asked between warmup shots.

Charley groaned. "Wrong question."

Jake nodded. "Yeah, Nancy mentioned there were new developments. So, is Casey going to leave Wilder or what?"

Charley fired the ball and sank a hook shot. "If I had my way. But I just don't understand her. She says she loves me and wants to marry me someday. So why can't that someday be now?"

Jake shrugged. "From the look of things, she seems pretty happy here. Getting into her classes and stuff."

"Yes, but you should have seen her in L.A.," Charley said. "She totally ruled that town. I never completely understood why she went away to school. She's a great actress."

"There are all sorts of reasons people want to go to college," Nick said, joining in.

"I know, I know," Charley said. "She needs to explore other interests. Things she wants to study."

"If she doesn't want to act," Jake wondered aloud, "what else could she do in Hollywood?"

Charley sighed. "That's exactly what I'm worried about. What if she decides she doesn't want to act? Would she want to go back to L.A.?"

"Well, you're still going to be there, right?" Jake replied.

Charley eyed him, wondering if he could really trust him. "Let me ask you guys a question. Casey's beautiful, right?"

Nick laughed. "Is that a trick question?" he asked, amazed.

"Okay," Charley continued, "so how long is it going to take before some great-looking guy here at Wilder comes along and sweeps her off her feet?"

Holding the ball, Jake said, "First of all, if she loves you, she'll come back to be with you."

"Yeah," Nick added. "Why pick a college guy over a movie star like you?"

"Charley," Jake said, shaking his head, "I'm kind of blown away. I didn't know that famous people were so insecure."

Charley leveled his gaze at Jake and repeated his question: "What if she doesn't want to come back?"

Jake nodded. "So you're trying to get her to

marry you now so she can't say no later, is that it? Look, I don't know Casey as well as you do, but I'd trust her a little more than that."

Nick cleared his throat. "Excuse me for saying so," he began, "but it sounds like you want Casey to do all the sacrificing for your relationship."

Charley was silent. "Thanks," he finally said. "I guess I need to think about that."

Suddenly, the ball was shoved into his chest.

"Enough psychology for one day," Jake proclaimed. "How about a little game of cutthroat two-on-one? Okay, Charley, there's the ball, there's the basket. Forget your troubles, and get into gear!"

CHAPTER 9

"So are we all set for tonight?" Casey asked. She looked down at the list of supplies the Kappas had gathered for their attack on the Zeta house. Holly Thornton, the Kappa vice president, tossed the last of the supplies they'd bought into a big black garbage bag. There were tons of old newspapers and rolls of packing tape and the glue tubes they'd found at the hardware store downtown.

"We're set." Holly grinned, flopping down onto the big couch in the Kappa living room. "I just *love* this idea. It was pure genius."

Casey laughed. "Take a bow, Bess."

"Thanks, Holly," Bess said, bending forward. "But do you think you can tell that 'pure genius' part to any of my professors?"

"It would definitely raise your grade-point average," Casey said, chuckling.

"Everyone knows where to meet, right?" Bess asked excitedly. "Holly, you're bringing the other Kappas to Thayer, where we'll all meet in the lobby."

"Three A.M., on the dot," Holly agreed.

"Thank goodness for crew practice." Eileen laughed, perching herself on the arm of the couch. "I'm *almost* used to getting up that early."

"You mean staying up that late," Bess corrected.

Casey was listening to the jokes and banter of her friends, but her spirit wasn't in it. She was still thinking about Charley's proposal. So far, Charley's visit hadn't made Casey's decision any easier. She'd been hoping that if they were face-to-face, all the questions would be answered and they'd both know exactly what to do. But the truth was that being face-to-face meant there was room for even more misunderstandings.

Casey had been waiting all day to see her sorority sisters so she could get their opinions on the situation. It didn't seem there would be a better time, so she just plunged in.

"Now that we're done with the house business," Casey began, "I have something I need to discuss." She sighed. "I need some advice about my situation with Charley."

Casey's three friends were all sitting on the couch, their eyes riveted to her.

"We've been dying to give you advice," Holly said.

"We didn't want to pry," Eileen added.

"But we *are* your friends," Bess pointed out. "And we don't want you to leave," she lamented. Holly and Eileen nodded.

Casey burst out laughing. It felt so good to have something to laugh about. She'd been thinking so hard about Charley and marriage that she hadn't realized how much it was weighing on her. What great friends she had, Casey thought.

"Now that you know what *we* want," Holly said, "ignore us and talk."

"Well, knowing how you feel," Casey teased, "I can pretty well guess what you're going to say: Stay here no matter what."

"No," Bess insisted, shaking her head. "We want what's best for *you,* Casey."

"I realize people say you're supposed to wait and everything, and not rush into marriage," Casey said.

"They do bill it as a forever kind of commitment thing," Eileen agreed.

"Right." Casey nodded. "So I don't want to do it too fast or too soon. But what about love?"

Holly grinned knowingly. "What about it?"

"Well, I love Charley," Casey said. "I know I do. So why should I wait?"

"First of all," Eileen said, "there's no such thing as 'supposed to' or 'shouldn't.' "

"The important question is what you want," Bess said. "About school, I mean. Isn't that why you left Hollywood in the first place?"

"I know," Casey admitted. "But am I just being stubborn? I could take classes anywhere if I really wanted to."

"Sure," Bess agreed, grinning. "But anywhere wouldn't have us."

"That's true," Casey said dryly. "Which only makes me wonder why I'd want to stay here."

Instantly, Casey had three couch cushions in her face.

"Kidding—kidding," she said, coming up for air. "Look, most of the trouble I'm having about making up my mind is because of you guys and my other friends. I really like it here. But what if I decide to stay and I lose Charley?"

"Why would you lose him?" Holly asked.

"I don't know," Casey answered, running a hand through her hair. "Because maybe he won't want to wait. Four years is a long time. And what if he doesn't want me four years from now?" Casey paused.

"Wait a minute," Eileen finally said, holding up her hand. "Let me get this straight: instead of finding out what you really want to do, you'd rather give it up, just to make sure that what you really want isn't something he really doesn't want?" Eileen asked, wrinkling her brow in confusion. "Is that what you mean?"

"Exactly," Casey said with a firm nod.

"Does that even make sense?" Bess asked.

"But what if I can't have both? What if I have to choose now, Charley or school? What do I choose?"

"Listen," Bess cut in. "Don't you remember the advice you gave me?"

"Was it good?" Casey asked, wincing.

"Yes," Bess laughed. "It was good. Remember when I felt bad about wanting to focus on myself instead of spending time with Paul? You told me I had to be together for myself before I could give some of myself to some guy."

"I said that?" Casey smiled, proud of herself. "Really?"

"Surprising, isn't it?" Eileen joked. "But you really do know what the right thing to do is. And Casey, I've seen Charley around you enough to know that he really loves you."

"Of course he does," Holly agreed. "Why else would he ask you to marry him?"

"You have to take care of yourself first," Eileen added.

"And, anyway, it's not an all-or-nothing thing, is it?" Bess asked. "I mean, if he really cares about you, he'll wait."

117

Casey bit her lip and nodded slowly. "That's what I want to believe," Casey admitted. "But will he?" she wondered nervously.

"Thank you again, Miss Drew," the voice on the other end of the line said. "If we need anything more, we'll give you a call." There was a click, and Nancy hung up the phone, irritated. "Of course," she muttered to herself. "You have my number."

Nancy had just spent another fifteen minutes on the phone with one of the detectives investigating the lab fire. She'd been over her story with them so many times that Nancy knew the detective was only pretending to have more questions to ask her about the fire the other night. All he really wanted to do was make her go through her story again—for about the fortieth time.

He's just trying to get me to contradict myself, Nancy knew, to see if I forgot something or added a new detail. Common things among guilty people.

"But I'm *not* guilty!" she said in exasperation.

Just then there was a knock. Nancy pushed her chair back from her desk, sighed, and went to open the door.

"Hi." Jake stood there, smiling. Before Nancy could even say anything, Jake brushed past her into the room. "Listen," he began, "we never had a chance to talk. I thought that maybe now would be a good time—"

"Well, then, you were wrong," Nancy blurted out.

Jake stopped in his tracks. "Nancy?" he asked, turning back to her, the expression on his face full of concern. "Is something wrong? What happened?"

"What happened?" Nancy said. "I just got off the phone with the police!" she cried. "That detective we spoke to called me again. Just to go over the 'facts' of our story—again. Just to see if I would get it right—again!"

"Oh, Nancy," Jake said sadly. "I'm sorry."

"Really?" Nancy asked. "Look, I know no one forced me to do anything. I went to the lab with you because I wanted to help. But all of this mess"—Nancy shrugged wearily—"the questioning, and the police suspecting us, all of this could have been avoided. We should have immediately told the police about Amy, Chaz, and Mike. I just want to know that you understand that."

"So, are you going to kick me out of your room right now?" Jake asked.

Nancy crossed her arms. She almost wanted to. Hadn't she decided she was going to worry about herself from now on? But the sight of him, of his adorable, troubled face and tousled hair, made it impossible for her. She just shook her head.

"Good." Jake sank down onto Nancy's bed. "Because I don't want this to ruin everything between us. That would be the worst thing that could happen."

"What about expulsion?" Nancy muttered. "That wouldn't exactly be a picnic, would it?"

"Of course not," Jake admitted. "But that's not going to happen."

"Why are you so sure?" Nancy asked. "Why shouldn't it happen? Look what's happened so far. I mean, I know it's not totally your fault."

"Thanks," Jake joked. "I guess that means you don't think *I* started the fire."

"But how can I not be upset?" Nancy asked. "If we hadn't tried to help those animal rights people, we wouldn't be in this mess." Nancy sighed and leaned against her desk.

"I guess I didn't think we could really get in trouble," Jake replied.

Instinctively, Nancy felt her heart warming. She knew how principled Jake was. She knew he hadn't meant for things to get so dangerous for them.

"And when I told you I wanted to try to talk to those guys myself, you were right there with me," Jake reminded her. "You trusted me. You just said where and when."

"I know," Nancy admitted, finally being honest with herself, too. "That's also why I'm so mad. It wasn't the best thing to do, but I agreed to it."

"Neither of us expected a burning laboratory," Jake pointed out gently.

"But I wasn't thinking straight," Nancy muttered. She heard her bed creaking. Without looking up, she knew that Jake had come to stand in front of her.

"That's one of the things I love about you," he whispered. "That you don't always think straight when I'm around. And that you did trust me." Nancy felt his warm hands come to rest on her shoulders.

"I hope I haven't lost that trust," Jake said, his breath ruffling her hair. "And I hope I can still confuse you. Even a little."

Nancy raised her head to answer, but she couldn't. Jake's lips were on hers before she could speak. It was a tender, gentle kiss, and Nancy was helpless against it. Her arms circled his waist, and she sagged against him. It felt so good to be held, and Jake's body was so sweetly familiar.

Finally, Jake pulled away a little.

"Nancy," he said, leaning his forehead against hers, "I know we have a lot of work to do to get ourselves out of this."

Nancy looked into his eyes. They were honest. Sincere. Caring. She nodded.

"But we can't help ourselves if we can't help each other," Jake continued. "We're in this together. And I know we can beat it."

"You're right," Nancy said softly, bringing

her hands to the sides of his face. "Two heads *are* better than one." She pulled Jake back toward her. "And so are two sets of lips."

The staccato sound of Stephanie's fingernails drumming on the counter rang through the little boutique. After getting off the phone with her father earlier that morning, she'd run right downtown with her credit cards, gone into a store, grabbed a shirt off the rack, and raced for the counter to buy it. But the first credit card she'd thrown down had been rejected.

Rejected! Stephanie had felt like dying of embarrassment. She'd quickly given the salesperson another card, and now Stephanie was waiting for her to ring it through the machine.

But she couldn't stop replaying her earlier conversation with her father. Stephanie had been so glad to hear from him. Of course, she hadn't admitted that right away. And she was glad she hadn't, after she heard what he had to say.

"Stephanie," he'd said, "you haven't lost your credit cards, have you?"

"Of course not," she'd replied, as she looked at the crumpled pile of shopping bags by her dresser.

"Well, then, I guess it's true," he'd said. "You're the one spending all this money."

At first Stephanie had thought he was joking. He used to complain about Stephanie's expensive tastes, and then lavish her with gift upon gift. But she'd been wrong. Very wrong.

"Kiki's been telling me I spoil you," he'd said, sending Stephanie into shock. "I hadn't wanted to agree with her, but now it looks as though she's right."

Kiki? My dreadful, thieving little stepmother? Right about me? Stephanie had wanted to scream, She doesn't even know me! But she'd managed to bite her tongue.

"I'm going to have to put a limit on your spending, Stephanie. Effective immediately. We'll talk about this later."

Great, Stephanie thought, shaking so hard she was afraid she might actually explode.

"Excuse me, miss?"

Stephanie looked up. The salesperson was standing in front of her, a pinched expression on her face. "This second card you gave us doesn't seem to be working, either."

"What do you mean it's not working?" Stephanie demanded. "They were all working yesterday." She rifled through her bag until she saw a flash of shiny gold. Then she pulled out another card and slapped it on the counter. "Try this one, then."

"I'm sorry, miss," the saleswoman said. "But our policy is a two-card maximum—"

"I don't care about your policy!" Stephanie cried, her voice cracking. "I'm a customer. I want to buy. Just try the card!"

The woman backed away, shaking her head.

He's really done it, Stephanie thought. I can't believe he's really done it.

"I'm sorry," the woman replied. She pulled the shirt from Stephanie's hand. Then she slid the gold card back across the shiny black counter. "You're over the limit on this card. Just like all the others."

CHAPTER 10

Are you sure Bill Graham can help us?" Jake asked as he followed Nancy down the stairs to the second floor of Thayer Hall. He tossed her an apple. "Because I'm really hungry."

"We need to talk to someone at Health-Tech," Nancy replied. "Bill knows those people in the lab—maybe he can get us a name."

As Nancy knocked on Bill's door, Jake gave her a peck on the cheek. She felt as light as air; she never realized how much energy it took to stay mad at someone. But Jake had been such a big part of her life since she'd come to Wilder that life was really lonely without him— even for a few hours.

As the doorknob was turning, Nancy was

planting a kiss on Jake's lips. Bill caught the end of it.

"Are you selling those door-to-door?" he asked, grinning.

"You wish," Nancy said, and laughed, blushing. She cleared her throat. She was about to speak when Bill turned and said to someone in the room, "Here are two of those animal freedom fighters now."

Nancy shot Jake a worried look. Did Bill know they were suspects in the arson? Nancy heard footsteps, and the doorway filled with an older guy. He was short and stocky, with jet black hair and a well-trimmed black beard. "Yep," he said, narrowing his eyes. "I remember these two troublemakers. You were at the protest, weren't you?"

Nancy was confused. This guy seemed serious, but Bill was laughing.

"Relax, Nance," Bill said lightheartedly. "Tony and I were just talking about all the student resistance to the stuff we do at the lab. This is Tony Ricci. He works on the Health-Tech research."

"I did—until Sunday night," Tony said with a shrug, "when all my work from the last couple of years went up in smoke. Poof."

Nancy shook her head. "That's awful. I'm really sorry to hear it."

"Oh, sure," Tony said with a sarcastic laugh. "All of you animal rights people are probably glad. The sad thing is that you don't know everything that was going on in there. That was important work."

"We *are* sorry," Jake insisted. "Don't think we're all the same."

"Hey," Bill chimed in, "I'd be glad to have this wonderfully cheerful conversation in the hall, but why don't you guys come in? Looks like you're here about something important."

Nancy and Jake sat on Bill's bed. Tony leaned back on the desk, as Bill grabbed a chair to sit on.

"So you really lost all your research?" Nancy asked.

"The whole enchilada," Tony said with a sad laugh. "I've been tearing my hair out ever since the fire. The ironic thing is, we were getting no results in any of our HealthTech research for the longest time. Then suddenly, in the last six weeks, everything seemed to come together in Jeanette's work. Jeanette Rigaud is the grad student in charge of the research, and she was working on a major part of the project. She tallied her recent findings, and all of a sudden, there it was. Success! Everything we'd hoped for in this part of the project actually looked like it was going to work. It was a major step in completion of the HealthTech research."

"Then the fire," Jake threw in.

"And now all that's gone," Nancy concluded.

Bill looked at Tony. "Not all," he said.

"Yes," Tony continued. "Luckily, Jeanette had made copies of her most recent reports a few days before the fire. So all the hard data was saved."

"So you won't have to redo all the experiments," Nancy concluded.

Tony nodded. "So *she's* happy, of course."

"But you're not. Why?" Nancy asked.

"Because," Bill answered, "since Jeanette made copies of her research reports, she has everything she needs to get her Ph.D. at the end of the year."

"But not me," Tony added with a sigh. "And neither do a lot of other grad students. It'll take us months to replicate all our findings. And Jeanette's news about her success in the research has just led to her getting a job offer from HealthTech. She can continue all of her work there. All she needs is her degree."

"Jeanette," Nancy repeated to herself.

Bill raised an eyebrow. "So you know her?"

Nancy looked at Jake. "Not really." But I'd like to get to know her better, she thought to herself. Too many things keep coming back to her, she realized. First, she knows about there being three people in the lab Sunday night. Now she seems to have saved her own research data just in the nick of time. Things are turning out too well for her and too badly for everyone else.

* * *

"Okay." Bess took a big breath. She was finally seated at her desk with her books in front of her. She was ready to do battle with her homework.

"So what if it's almost midnight?" she muttered. "The night is young. And I have to be up in three hours, anyway. Why bother going to bed?"

She cracked open her Western civ textbook. She had to read twenty pages and write a summary.

"Causes of World War I," she tried to read with enthusiasm. But by the time she reached the end of the sentence, she sighed. She eyed the bottle of soda at the far end of the desk. "Well, okay, maybe just a quick soda break. Then I'll *really* get into this."

Finally, her glass full, she started to read. But before she finished the first paragraph, the door flew open, and there stood Leslie. She was wearing one of Bess's favorite fall outfits, her long black wool skirt and a flowered angora sweater Bess had bought in a used-clothing store. Bess was stunned. Leslie in *her* clothes? Though I have to admit, Bess thought, she does look really pretty in them.

And was that Bess's makeup on her face? Her lipstick looked kind of smudged. Evidence of romance, maybe?

What had she been up to? Bess wondered. "Well, hello there," she said.

Leslie leaned back against the closed door, grinning—and not saying a word.

"I guess this means you and Nathan had a good time?"

Leslie pushed herself away from the wall, faced the mirror, and undid her ponytail. "We went to a movie," she said.

"And?" Bess asked.

"We went to dinner," Leslie added obliquely.

Bess was nodding. "Okay. Movie and dinner. Then?"

"We went for a walk."

"Wow, a walk!" Bess deadpanned.

A little grin appeared on Leslie's face. "I think I really like him."

Bess inspected her roommate closely. There was something very different about her. She was eerily calm. She was serene. So, Bess thought, this is Leslie in happy mode. Very nice.

Suddenly, Leslie whirled around. "But do you think he likes *me?* I mean, he said he did, and he asked me out again for this weekend."

Bess nodded. "All signs that he likes you."

"And we went up to his place—"

Bess held up her hands. "Whoa there, girl! *His* place? He took you up to *his* place? Already?"

Leslie was blushing. She nodded, blotting her lipstick. "But nothing happened."

"Oh," Bess said, disappointed, and sagged back into her chair.

"Though he kissed me when I left."

Bess looked interested again. "Tell me everything!"

But that was Bess's first mistake. Because Leslie opened her mouth and didn't close it for an entire half hour. She gave Bess every detail of her date with Nathan. What he said, then what she said, what she was thinking, what she thought he was thinking.

By the time Leslie was done, Bess's eyes were at half-mast, and she was actually throwing longing glances at her Western civ textbook, cringing at the thought of going into class the next day totally unprepared.

Any change for the better in Leslie, she remembered telling George. Well, now she wasn't so sure. For the first time since Bess had known Leslie, she actually wished her roommate would shut up and study!

"Ow!" Eileen cried as she stumbled her way across the room in the dark.

"Wha—" Reva moaned, raising her head off her pillow. "Who's there?"

"Shhh," Eileen whispered. "Go back to sleep. It's three in the morning."

Reva groggily sat up, pulling at her flannel nightgown. "What are you doing up?"

"Nothing. Go back to sleep," Eileen said.

Hands out in front of her, she staggered toward the door—or at least what she thought was the door. But the only light in the room was from the alarm clock, and the little green numbers didn't light up anything. Stepping, turning, she reached for the doorknob. "Ouch!" She pulled the door into her foot.

Out in the hall, there was only dead silence and darkness. Eileen headed for the bathroom to brush her teeth. "Where's that light?" she asked, feeling the wall for the switch. She found a bump and fingered it, but instead of the light, the fan inside the bathroom went on, whirling and knocking and wheezing. "Shh," she cried, struggling to find the switch to turn it off. Shuffling her feet to steady herself, she kicked square into something hard, metallic, and loud—the trash can.

Doors up and down the hall were opening. Someone turned on the hall light.

Eileen hid her face, not sure whether to laugh or cry. "I'd make a terrible spy," she muttered.

"What's going on?" It was Nancy, coming out of her room in underwear and a T-shirt. Stephanie stalked toward her wearing her slinky silk nightie.

"What . . . are . . . you . . . doing?" Stephanie yelled. She dangled a watch in Eileen's face. "Do you know what time it is?"

Kara and then Ginny and Liz came in yawning and stretching. Everyone started talking at once.

"Okay, okay," Eileen said, her hands raised. "If you all *must* know, the Kappas are about to unleash their plan of revenge on the Zeta—"

There was a soft knock on the suite door, and the entire suite of girls moved toward the lounge, where Eileen opened the door. Holly, Bess, and two other Kappa sisters were standing there clutching pillowcases bulging with supplies.

"I want to come," Kara said.

Nancy started to snicker. "Me, too. This looks like fun."

"Nan," Bess said, shaking her head, "you know you can't."

"I can't believe you didn't tell me, your own roommate!" Reva cried, coming out buckling her belt. "I'll organize a mutiny if we can't all come."

"Where's Casey?" Eileen asked.

Casey, in black jeans and a black T-shirt, appeared in the lounge. "Here I am, ready and willing."

Eileen herded everyone else back toward their rooms. "Sorry, this is a Kappa exclusive," she warned. "Go find your own group of guys to terrorize!"

"This is fun!" Bess whispered as she and the other Kappas rounded the corner to Fraternity

Row. Bess had a sack over her shoulder filled with rolls of packing tape. Eileen and Holly Thornton carried either end of a long ladder. Casey cradled stacks of newspapers. Soozie Beckerman and the other five Kappa women carried large tubes of water-soluble glue.

"It is okay what we're doing, isn't it?" Eileen asked in a moment of weakness.

Bess swallowed her laughter. "Okay? Let me tell you something. Those guys sleeping in there," she said, pointing to the Zeta house coming up on their left, "deserve everything we're about to give them."

Holly piped up, "Women, it's time. Do we all have our assignments?"

Bess took one last look at the Zeta house as she knew it. It was a beautiful stone mansion with turrets and towers.

"Let's do it," Bess said with relish.

They fanned out in the night. Quietly, they spread newspaper over the windows on the first two floors, then sealed the tall windows with layers of industrial tape. Bess, armed with a caulking gun, aimed the tip into the locks on the front and back doors, packing them with water-soluble glue—it wouldn't ruin the doors, but it would take a lot of work, hours and hours of it, to remove.

A half hour later, Bess, Eileen, and Holly were standing side by side, looking up at the front of the house. Bess clucked her tongue. "Poor boys."

"I hope they have enough food to last until tomorrow," Eileen said with mock sadness. "What about their classes? What about football practice?"

"They can always jump off one of the turrets on the upper floor," Bess said, laughing.

CHAPTER 11

The second Kara opened her eyes, she was wide awake. The clock in front of her read 6:59.

Slipping out of bed, she was in the bathroom brushing her teeth in record time. Back in her room, she gathered up the materials she'd found at the psych department: flashcards with funny shapes on one side and various explanations on the other.

I have to try this stuff out before I use any of it on Montana, Kara thought, eyeing Nancy's bed. She flipped to the page in the book where it gave testing instructions: "Subjects should be tested when they're most receptive; for instance, the first thing in the morning."

Kara tiptoed over to Nancy's bed. "Hey, Nancy?" Kara asked softly.

"Wha—" Nancy moaned, tugging down the blanket.

"Are you awake?" Kara asked.

Eyes shut, Nancy raised an eyebrow. She moaned again. "I wasn't," Nancy managed to mumble through the covers.

"But you are now, right?" Kara prodded.

"No." Nancy put her head back under the covers.

"That's great," Kara continued, ignoring her answer. "Because I just need to ask you one little thing. But you have to open your eyes."

Nancy shook her head under the blanket. "Too early," she said.

Kara nudged her. "Just one little second. For me, your loyal roommate?"

Nancy brought her head out and unstuck one eye, then the other. "Okay, they're open. What?"

Kara dangled the flashcard inches from Nancy's nose. The testing instructions said the element of surprise was essential—spontaneity was a must. "Tell me what you see," Kara ordered. "Tell me what this looks like. The first thing that comes to mind. Don't think. Quick!"

Nancy blinked, sighed, yawned. "It—um,

well, Kara, it looks a lot like an ink blot on
a flashcard."

Snorting, Kara straightened up. "You're
so—so—literal!"

"And asleep," Nancy added, burrowing back
under her blankets.

Sighing, Kara bolted out of the room, armed
with her deck of cards. She heard water running in the bathroom and headed for the door.
Reva was doubled over the sink, splashing
water on her face.

"Reva," Kara said. "Quick, what do you
see?"

Reva slowly raised her head. "Kara, what in
the world?" she said crankily.

"Just tell me what you see," Kara said
again. "Please!"

"Look, we were all up really late last night.
I have an early computer lab. Don't do this to
me right now."

"It'll just take a sec," Kara said cheerily.
"Come on, be a pal. Just tell me what you see.
And don't think too hard. Just the first thing
that crosses your mind."

Reva crossed her arms and closed one eye
threateningly. "Read my lips. Good ... bye."
She gently pushed Kara out of the bathroom
and slammed the door.

Balancing a cup of coffee and a doughnut
on her knee, Nancy drove her Mustang slowly

through campus and into a neighborhood of modest houses on the fringe of the university. She'd been holding herself back all morning. All she wanted to do when she got up was run over to Jeanette Rigaud's house. Tony had given her the address.

But Nancy didn't want to cause suspicion by showing up too early. So she'd sat in her room, trying to focus on a list of questions for her upcoming interview with Mrs. Vandenbrock. But the second the clock struck ten-thirty, Nancy was on her way down to her car.

Jeanette Rigaud's house was a small, shingled ranch on the edge of campus. Nancy knew this was the part of town where many of Wilder's grad students lived. A lot of grad students worked at part-time jobs to make ends meet, or lived on small stipends they got from the university.

It's kind of interesting that Jeanette Rigaud has such a nice car, Nancy thought as she noticed the back of a red sports car in the garage. I wonder if she has family money.

When the grad student answered the door, Nancy could tell she wasn't exactly ecstatic to see her. The smile on her face was strained. "Oh, hi."

"Nancy, remember?"

"Sure." Jeanette Rigaud nodded uncertainly. "So, what's up?"

"I'm still working on that story." Nancy

smiled, waving her notebook. "I had some more questions. To be honest, your research sounded really interesting. I just wanted to hear some more about it. Could you spare a few minutes?"

Jeanette glanced at her watch and shrugged. "Well, I really don't have much time. If it's only for a few minutes, okay. Come on in." She stepped back to let Nancy through the door. "Though I don't know what more I can tell you," she went on. "My research results are sealed until HealthTech is ready to go public."

Nancy and Jeanette Rigaud sat on frayed, overstuffed chairs. Glancing around quickly, Nancy could see that the house was furnished with odds and ends from thrift shops and yard sales. No family money here, Nancy decided.

"That's okay," Nancy said. "I'm more interested in the human-interest angle anyway. What's it like working in a lab?"

"It's just a regular lab," Jeanette said evasively. "Animals and beakers and stuff."

"But you must work hard, lots of late nights?" Nancy asked.

Jeanette Rigaud shrugged. "Sure. I'm sometimes there all night."

"And your job offer from HealthTech?" Nancy asked casually. "You must really be looking forward to working there, after all you've done on their project here at Wilder."

The grad student narrowed her eyes. "How did you find out about my job offer?"

"It was something someone mentioned in passing." Nancy waited for a reaction. Jeanette Rigaud looked up at the clock, then out the window. Her eyes scanned the sparsely furnished room. Nervous, maybe? Nancy wondered. "People say all sorts of things in interviews," she said.

"It seems as though it will be a terrific job," the other woman finally said. "I was lucky to get the offer."

"Sounds like more than luck," Nancy said meaningfully. "Sounds like you earned it."

Jeanette Rigaud blushed. "I guess things have gone pretty well at the lab lately—"

"Until the fire," Nancy cut in.

"Of course!" Jeanette replied quickly. "It's a terrible blow to lose so much research. Though, thank goodness, the results from my part of the project were saved."

Nancy nodded. "I heard that, too. That *was* lucky. You know, I thought it was kind of interesting, when I spoke to you the other day, that you didn't mention that it was your office that was burned."

"I have no idea why those radicals targeted my office," Jeanette sputtered. "They don't know the damage they've done! Even though

141

I had copies of my final results, I still could have used my research notes. And I had the research from other parts of the project, the work of the other grad students. And those poor animals. They could have been killed, too!"

Nancy agreed. "And I guess it's just lucky for the university—and for HealthTech—that your findings on the project didn't get destroyed."

"You know," Jeanette said, standing and picking up her purse and car keys. "I really have to get going now. Would you mind?"

"Of course not," Nancy replied, following her out of the house and into the garage. "So, when did you say you were starting at Health-Tech?" she asked.

"I didn't," Jeanette Rigaud said tightly.

As Nancy walked with her to the front of the garage, the cuff of her jeans caught on a plastic crate labeled Weston Recycles! The box was full of bottles, cans, and plastic containers. A few of the bottles on top were filled with clear liquid. Nancy tripped, and a bottle rolled off and crashed to the floor, splashing her pants and spreading along the cement.

Jeanette Rigaud ran over and kicked the glass away.

"Wow, I'm really sorry," Nancy said, bending to clean it up.

"Forget it," the grad student said. "I'll get

it when I get home. I really have to leave now, so if you don't mind . . ."

"I got some on my pants," Nancy noticed.

Jeanette Rigaud bent to look. "You'll want to wash those as soon as you get home," she said insistently. "That stuff is really strong paint thinner—you won't want to breathe it. And the smell will get all over your other clothes if you leave your pants lying around."

Nancy nodded. "No problem. I'm really sorry."

The grad student nodded. "I absolutely have to leave now."

"Well, thanks for the interview."

"Sure," Jeanette Rigaud said curtly. "Just don't forget about those pants."

"Right," Nancy replied under her breath.

Lying in bed, Bess thought of all the Western civ homework she didn't get done last night. Or the night before. Or the night before that . . .

"But I did get something done," she thought, smiling.

It was late morning, and Leslie was long gone, off to class. Bess's eyes fluttered closed. Gleefully, she pictured her favorite Zeta, Paul, checking his watch as he was running toward the door, possibly late for class. He turns the knob. Nothing. Turns again. The door doesn't budge.

Bess chuckled sleepily and began to drift

happily away. The distant ring of a telephone right by her ear hauled her back to an awake state. Bess snatched the phone.

"Guess who?"

Bess fell back in bed and laughed. "Why, I have no idea."

"I think you've been a busy girl," the voice said with a menacing sort of sweetness.

"Oh, Paul, it's *you,*" Bess replied, her tone all innocence and light. "I didn't recognize your voice. Why are you calling so early?"

"Well, I had this idea," Paul began, "to surprise you and take you out for breakfast. But I can't."

"Why?" Bess said. "I'd *love* to go out to breakfast."

"It seems that I can't get out of my house," Paul explained.

Bess faked a gasp. "But what do you mean you can't get out?"

"Well," Paul replied thoughtfully, "it seems the doors are a little slow to open. The windows, too, for some reason."

Bess could hardly contain her laughter. "Did you try the third-floor windows? I'm sure they would work."

"A little high," Paul said, "though there is that tree I could try to leap for. Of course, if I missed . . ."

"Ew!" Bess cringed. "Then I guess I'll be eating breakfast without you. I sure do wish

I could help. Actually, I do know the names of some big, strong fellows who might be able to break down the door to the house if you like."

Bess could hear Paul breathing. "Okay, smarty," he said. "Just wait till I get my hands on you."

"Mmmmm." Bess sighed. "Sounds good. I'm waiting. . . ."

Click.

Laughing, Bess put down the phone. "That should give him some incentive," she said, and settled under her comforter for a long, warm sleep.

"So, needless to say, she wasn't exactly happy to see me," Nancy relayed as she sat heavily on her bed.

Jake was pacing in the middle of her room. Nancy had called him after her interview with Jeanette Rigaud and told him to meet her back at her dorm. "You always said there was something about her you couldn't put your finger on."

Nancy noticed a piece of paper on Kara's bed. "Hey, what's that?" She nodded toward the bed.

Jake picked it up and handed it to her. The note was in Kara's unintelligible scrawl: "Vandenbrock. Appointment Friday 10 A.M. *sharp* (she said if you're late, don't bother showing up)."

"Excellent!" Nancy said.

As Nancy read, Jake sniffed the air. "What's that awful smell?"

Nancy sniffed. "Whew, that does stink. When I was at Jeanette Rigaud's, I tripped and knocked over a bottle that broke. It had some kind of liquid in it and it splashed on my jeans. She said it was paint thinner. Wait a second!" Nancy sniffed again. She crouched down and smelled the side of her leg. "Take a whiff of this, and tell me if it reminds you of anything."

Jake leaned over closer to her leg. "It does remind me of something, but what?"

"Try the fire," Nancy replied. "That funny chemical smell."

Jake's mouth opened, but nothing came out. "That stuff was at Jeanette's?"

Nancy thought a minute. "It sure was. And so were a few other bottles of it." Nancy's eyes locked on Jake's. "Are you thinking what I'm thinking?"

Jake sat back on Kara's bed. "Okay," he said, his eyes alight. "Who do we know who knows about chemicals?" He snapped his fingers. "Bill Graham!"

But Nancy was smiling. "I know someone better. Someone who knows chemicals *and* who knows that lab."

Jake pointed at her. "Yes! Good! Tony Ricci!"

Nancy already had the student directory in her hands. She circled a number and dialed.

"Tony!" she said excitedly. "I'm glad you're home. This is Nancy Drew, from the other day. I have a question for you."

Five minutes later she replaced the phone gently in its cradle and shook her head.

Jake stared at her. "What? Tell me!"

"Well," Nancy began, "it seems that during the experiments, Tony, Jeanette, and the others were using a particular chemical called"—Nancy glanced at the notepad where she had written the name—"triethyl-glyceride. It's used a lot in pharmaceutical research. But they stopped using it more than a year ago."

"Oh," Jake said, disappointed. "So it's a dead end?"

Nancy shook her head. "Tony said Jeanette brought what was left home with her to continue some experiments. Tony said he didn't like it, but since Jeanette had worked with the chemical, he knew she'd handle and store it properly. And she was in charge, so there wasn't much he could say about it, anyway."

"Why would she need to be so careful with it?" Jake asked.

Nancy stood up and took a step toward Jake. "Because"—she kissed him lightly—"it's extremely flammable."

"Flam—?"

She kissed him again. "Yes. All it would take to start a fire would be a single, small heat source."

Jake smiled. "Like a match?"

"Exactly."

CHAPTER 12

Nancy and Jake were hurrying across the quad to the *Wilder Times* offices. "Why do we have to do this *now?*" Nancy complained.

"It'll only take a second," Jake replied. "I want to make sure Gail gave me something better than filler blurbs for next week."

Inside, the offices were bustling. Phones were ringing, computer keyboards clicking.

Nancy found Jake staring at the story assignments on the bulletin board.

"So did she dump us?" Nancy asked blithely.

But Jake only nodded wordlessly.

"You're kidding!" Nancy gasped. "No way!" Looking at the board, Nancy couldn't find her or Jake's name on the assignment board.

A door opened and closed behind them. Gail hurried out holding a mockup for Monday's edition in her hands. It was only Thursday. That meant extra effort was going into the paper. The headline story, whatever it was, was going to be big.

"Gail," Jake began.

"You two are suspended until this thing is cleared up. I'm sorry, but I don't have a choice. This came from Dan," Gail said, looking distressed. She was referring to Dan McCall, the journalism professor who was the staff editorial advisor for the newspaper. "I'm late for an interview. I have to get going."

Buttonholing Gail, Nancy lowered her voice. "Does this mean our names are going to be in the paper?"

"Here," Gail said, shoving the mockup in her hands. "This is Monday's page one. You might find it interesting." Gail took off through the doors.

Nancy and Jake pored over the paper. The lead article was on the fire. The first two paragraphs related how two more students had been arrested for breaking into the lab. A few days after the fire, they were caught red-handed by the police unloading the stolen lab animals from a van into an animal shelter in the next town. The university was still deciding about pressing formal charges against the students, but it was decided they were going to be expelled.

"They're goners," Jake said when he read Amy's, Chaz's, and Mike's names in the article.

Nancy swallowed hard as she read on. "The administration is saying they aren't the last of the expulsions, Jake," she said fearfully, letting her arm drop with the rest of the article.

"But we didn't do anything," Jake asserted, still refusing to believe they were in real trouble.

"Look," Nancy insisted, "this is really bad for us. Chaz, Mike, and Amy aren't denying the break-in, or even that they stole the animals. But they continue to deny they set the fire. The police are probably still looking at them *and* at us. And we're pretty certain we know who did it."

"Jeanette," Jake said.

"Jeanette," Nancy agreed.

Jake shook his head. "But what could possibly be her motive? Her whole life was in that lab—"

"And it started in her office," Nancy agreed. "I don't know why, but we've got to tell the police what we know, especially about that glyceride stuff. *Now!*"

Stephanie flicked a match at the mirror, where it ricocheted and fell burning to the floor. "I *can't* believe it!" she sputtered, glaring at herself.

"I'll get her back, I'll get her back," she seethed, wishing she hadn't already torn up her picture of Kiki so she could tape it to her wall and watch it burn. "She got him to cancel my credit cards, I'm sure of it. He never would have thought of it by himself!"

All day she'd lain in bed wide awake, staring at the ceiling, waiting for some brilliant plan of revenge to come to her. She'd finally been unable to stand it and had lit up a cigarette.

"Now what am I going to do?"

"Open the windows, for one," Casey remarked from her side of the room. "Will you please stop smoking in here? Go to the lounge."

Stephanie shot her an evil stare. So, her roommate was sneaking up on her, too?

Casey cocked her head, pursed her lips, and considered her for a few long seconds. "Let me guess. You maxed out your credit cards?"

Stephanie was startled. "So what if I did?" she snapped, angrily putting out her cigarette. "It's not a federal case."

Casey laughed. "Believe me, I know. It's no fun. When I got my first big part in L.A., I went out and bought ten grand's worth of clothes."

Stephanie sniffed. "I'm not surprised."

Casey leveled a steady gaze at her. "So, no

money, huh? And I bet you have a huge debt, too."

Stephanie shrugged. "My father says I have to pay it all back," she whined.

"How dare he?" Casey asked, laughing. "I mean, it's not like they're his cards or anything."

Stephanie's face stung as if Casey had slapped her across the cheek.

"Sorry to hear it," Casey offered, softening. "I've been there, too."

Stephanie turned away.

"Maybe," Casey ventured, "it's time to consider something drastic."

Stephanie started to reach for another cigarette, then, remembering Casey's plea, she grudgingly decided against the idea. "Like what?"

"Something really far out there, really unthinkable," Casey said dramatically.

Stephanie tossed her head. "Uh-huh?"

Casey smiled. "A job."

George was reading the mockup for next Monday's paper. Nancy, Jake, and Will were seated around her on the steps of Jamison Hall. Students were filing in and out of the doors on their way to dinner. But Nancy couldn't eat a thing. She and Jake had just spent the last hour down at the police station, and it hadn't exactly been a pleasurable experience.

"To be honest," Will said, "I don't blame the police for not believing you."

Jake shot him an angry stare. "Thanks for your support."

George rested a soothing hand on his shoulder. "Come on, Jake. Think about it. Jeanette was in charge of that program. It might make sense theoretically that she would have done it—"

"But not realistically," Nancy finished the thought, nodding. "She's right, Jake. We need more than a theory to get them to believe us. And we didn't give the police enough credit. They turned our story right around on us." She turned to George. "The detective wondered how we would know all that stuff about the chemical if we didn't start the fire."

"Crack detectives, those Weston cops," George said, trying to lighten things up.

Jake was zeroed in on the mystery. "Maybe it does seem kind of suspicious. But you'd think that the detective would have realized it couldn't have been a coincidence that we told him about triethyl-glyceride *before* he told us that the fire marshal identified it as the source of the fire. And I can't believe he actually had the gall to accuse us of trying to frame Jeanette!" he seethed.

Nancy could still picture the scene perfectly: the detective accusing them of the frame-up, and Jake's face going beet red with anger. But the police were the ones with the badges. She and Jake were just college students trying to dig themselves out of a hole.

She touched Jake's arm. "I'm sorry," she said lovingly. "I thought that going to the cops was a good idea, but I should have thought it through more. I guess I kind of blew it."

The evening was fading to night. It was getting harder and harder to see.

George held the paper up to the light hanging over the entrance to Jamison to finish reading the article. "Wow," she said. "Those three guys had their hearts in the right place, but they sure were bumblers. Mike is quoted here as saying that when the fire started, he tried to save what he thought might be research notes, by grabbing papers off tables and desks. He says he stuffed what he could into his backpack before he was knocked unconscious, but when he woke up, he wasn't able to find the backpack anywhere. He figured it must have burned, too." George shook her head. "Nice try," she commented.

Nancy nodded in commiseration. "It did seem pretty careless of him. . . ." Suddenly, she leapt to her feet.

"Nancy, what's wrong?" George asked.

"Jake!" Nancy cried. "We didn't finish reading that article! Did you hear what George just said?"

"Something about papers, so what?"

"Mike's backpack! When I was giving him mouth-to-mouth, you threw his backpack into the back of my car. I've been so distracted, and the back of the Mustang is such a pit, I didn't even notice it. It's been sitting there the whole time, and if Mike took anything from the lab—"

Jake was on his feet before she finished. Nancy grabbed his hand, and they took off.

"So, Montana," Tim was saying, "tell me again how you felt when your parents got divorced?"

"The *first* time?" Montana asked seriously.

"Montana?" Kara asked, wriggling her fingers to get her attention. They were all sitting in the lounge of the Pi Phi sorority.

Kara had arranged the interview with Montana so that she and Tim could start to gather hard data for their American family project. But she had something else in mind, too. While Tim had been feeding Montana serious questions, Kara stood over Tim's shoulder, holding up her flash cards for Montana to "read."

"And how did that feel, when your mother got divorced the *second* time?" Tim asked earnestly.

But before Montana could answer, Kara held a card in the air. This one had the number 17 written on it, but Kara showed Montana the blank back.

"Honestly?" Montana was explaining to Tim. "I was beginning to lose track of who my real parents were, or how many parents I had. Kara, that's a seventeen."

Kara turned the card over just to make sure. "You're really amazing. That's the tenth one in a row you've gotten right."

Tim spun around in his seat. "We do have a paper to write," he said bluntly. "Are you going to help?"

"But this is so much more interesting," Kara insisted. "Here, watch." She held up the blank back of a card that had squiggly lines on the front of it. And Montana, wrinkling her nose with concentration, described it exactly.

Kara, hands on hips, stared Tim down. "You're talking about divorce, but I've found someone who's really clairvoyant! It's so cool! Do you know how rare that is? Now, wouldn't that make a *much* more interesting paper?"

Tim turned back to Montana. "Okay, Ms. Smith, tell me in your own words how it feels to be the subject of an ESP experiment."

Was that a wink Montana just gave him? Kara wondered. She held up another card.

"Six, seven, eight, four," Montana said. "Well, Tim, let me tell you, there's much more to ESP and clairvoyance than meets the eye. Especially when you're just looking straight ahead."

Tim let out a single hoot, then stopped.

Montana was looking at him funny, as if they were stopping each other from laughing.

Something's weird, Kara thought. "What is wrong with you people?"

Tim and Montana couldn't hold it back. Throwing their heads back, they started laughing.

"Will you please tell me what's going on?" Kara demanded.

Tim pushed himself out of his chair and kissed Kara on the cheek.

"Look," he said, smiling.

Taking Kara by the shoulders, he turned her around to face the mirror hanging on the wall.

"Yes?" Kara asked.

"The mirror," Tim said slowly.

Kara gazed at her own reflection. She could see Montana grinning behind her.

"Okay, so I'm the world's biggest, silliest, most naive idiot," Kara said, blushing. "And you could sell me the Brooklyn Bridge or a plot of land in Idaho sight unseen."

"Kara," Montana said affectionately, reaching out her hand.

Looking at Montana, Kara shook her head and started to laugh. Tim and Montana joined in.

"So you're not so amazing," Kara howled at Montana.

"Only as amazing as you!" Montana said, laughing hysterically.

CHAPTER 13

Nancy and Jake raced across campus toward the student parking lot behind Thayer. They passed students on their way to the library and to dinner, or to the field house where she knew the Wilder basketball team was scrimmaging with a local college in a preseason game. She didn't know what the papers in Mike's backpack would tell her, but she was sure they were going to be the last piece of the puzzle.

Her Mustang sat in the dark at the edge of the lot. Leaning against it, out of breath, she dug for the keys and handed them to Jake. He climbed over the front seat and handed her the small leather backpack Nancy remembered from Sunday night.

She opened it and spread the contents on

the roof of her car. "Manila folders, measuring cups, a beaker," she listed.

"I guess he panicked and just grabbed anything he could on the way out," Jake said sadly, "trying to save stuff. He must have known they were going to get blamed for that fire."

Nancy was flipping through the folders. "I can't read this," she concluded, shaking her head. "All these graphs and charts—I don't know what they mean."

Jake lifted a folder up to the light. "Look here," he said, pointing to the margins of the page. "See these pencil markings? These look like some kind of corrections. The points on these graphs were moved to different spots. And these result numbers down here in the corner were definitely changed. Look, you can see the eraser marks."

Nancy stared off into the distance. Her breath hung before her in balloons of vapor in the cool air. "Hey, remember what Tony said about the test results suddenly being successful after Jeanette started tabulating them?"

Jake nodded. "Yeah, but we don't know that that's what this is."

Nancy shoved the folders and beakers back into the backpack. "You're right. We can't be sure. We have to show them to someone who can read them—like Tony."

Nancy ran back into her dorm to look

through the campus phone book. She found Tony's address and sprinted back out. Jake was waiting for her, clutching the backpack against his chest.

"He doesn't live far from Jeanette," she said, panting. "Let's go."

The next five minutes felt like hours as Nancy wound her way through campus and town. Finally, she slowed in front of a small house. Tony's porch light was on.

She and Jake hurried to the door and knocked impatiently.

"Hey there," Tony said when he finally opened the door. "What are you two doing here?"

"Sorry to barge in on you like this," Nancy said, "but we've got something we need you to look at."

"Sure," Tony said. "But you don't have to stay on the porch. Come on in."

Nancy and Jake stepped into the house. A few other students were lounging in front of the TV eating out of big bowls of popcorn. Tony led Nancy and Jake into the kitchen and closed the door.

"So what can I help you with?" he asked.

Nancy handed him the folders.

Tony opened one up and started looking through the papers. "Wait a minute!" he said when he recognized them. He looked at Jake and Nancy curiously. "Where did you get these?"

Nancy looked over his shoulder. "There really isn't time to explain. Can you just tell us what they are?"

"These are the results I was telling you about," he said, agitated. "I haven't actually seen them in months. I figured they went up in the fire."

Jake leaned in, pointing to the pencil corrections. "What are these?"

Tony held them up to the light. Nancy noticed him begin to frown. He held more corrections up to the light. He sat at the table with the folders and went through them all, his expression darkening.

Finally, Tony raised his head, his mouth a straight, grim line. "I knew it!" he fumed. "I never would have said it out loud, because people in academics accuse people of cheating all the time. I never wanted to play that game. But this . . ."

He spread his palms over the folder.

"Jeanette changed the results of her part of the project," Nancy concluded.

Tony nodded. "We weren't getting what we wanted," he explained, his eyes frozen in a distant, cold stare. "A year went by, two years, three, and still nothing. Jeanette has been working at Wilder for *five years,* trying to make this HealthTech grant pay off. The money was running out at the end of this year. And she didn't want only her Ph.D., she wanted a big-time job at a big-time university, or at a company like HealthTech. HealthTech offered her that and more, but she had to give them what they wanted first, and they wanted *this*." He jabbed at the folders.

"And she would have done anything to get that," Nancy added.

"Anything," Tony agreed.

"Including falsifying the data?" Jake asked.

Tony laughed somberly. "It happens all the time. You only hear about it when people get caught."

Nancy sat heavily. "So she started the fire with that chemical to destroy the incriminating papers."

"In fact," Tony said, shaking his head, amazed, "one of the firefighters said that the stuff that burned first was manila folders. I bet that pile was her entire stack of evidence."

"But Mike was able to save these," Jake concluded. He stood. "She had everything to lose if anyone ever found the research notes that prove the *real* results."

Nancy grabbed her car keys. "But now someone has."

Before Casey was finished knocking on the door of Charley's room at the Collegetown

Motel, it flew open. Charley's lean, muscular frame filled the doorway. The lamp behind him made a halo of light around his thick black hair. I think he's beautiful, Casey thought as she stepped into the room and planted a hard kiss on his mouth. "There's more where that came from," she said, brushing past him.

"We need to talk," he said, closing the door behind him.

Casey scanned the room. Charley's suitcase was packed. She noticed his plane ticket sticking out of his jacket pocket. "You're leaving tonight?" she asked, wide-eyed. Suddenly, her mouth went dry. "But you're supposed to stay through the weekend."

Charley took her hand and sat her on the edge of the bed. "I've been doing a lot of thinking," he said.

"So have I, and I have my answer about getting married now," Casey said quickly.

But before Casey could finish getting the word *no* out of her mouth, Charley said no himself.

"What do you mean, no?" Casey asked, totally befuddled. "You're the one who proposed."

Charley shook his head sadly. "I was trying to give you space, like you wanted. I don't want to lose you to some college guy, but I know the answer isn't to do something neither of us is ready for. We need to be on the same page, so we can make a decision together."

Casey gazed at him. Her voice was hushed with amazement. "You didn't say any of this before."

"I just figured it out," Charley explained. "Sounded good, didn't it?"

Casey held his gaze. "That wasn't just a little monologue you came up with, was it? You meant that, right?"

Charley held up his right hand. "Cross my heart."

Casey fell back on the bed, relieved, and pulled Charley down with her. "We're having fun now, aren't we?" she said, gazing lovingly into his eyes. "I mean, you there, and me here, it's good for both of us."

Charley nodded. "We love each other," he said. "We just have to work hard." His expression turned serious. He sat up and took her hand in both of his.

"Casey, will you marry me—in four years?"

Casey swallowed. In a weird way, this *was* romantic. All this time, Charley was just a confused pile of mush, not the insensitive, stubborn guy she was afraid he was becoming. She loved him. She loved him so much.

"Yes, and I promise," Casey said, gazing

into his eyes, "that in four years, I will say yes again. Yes, Charley, I will marry you."

Walking up to Jeanette Rigaud's front door, Nancy and Jake didn't say a word. Even though Tony had said that cheating and changing results happened all the time in scientific research, doing something as dangerous as lighting a fire to cover yourself was much worse—someone had almost been killed.

Nothing's that important, she thought as she rapped on the door.

When Jeanette opened it, her face fell at the sight of Nancy. "I'm on my way out," she said.

"Well, this shouldn't take long," Nancy replied, and walked past her into the living room.

"You can't just barge into someone's house," Jeanette complained, her voice laced with anger.

"And you can't just burn a lab down," Jake shot back.

Jeanette looked stunned. "What is he talking about?" she demanded to know, looking at Nancy.

Nancy held up the folders. "These. We know everything, Jeanette."

Jeanette laughed patronizingly. "You wouldn't understand anything in those folders."

"We didn't have to," Nancy said. "Tony Ricci explained them to us."

Jeanette's eyes widened in fear.

Nancy continued, "I'm curious to know how these pages compare with the report you presented to HealthTech."

Jeanette's lips narrowed with spite. "Get out of my house, or I'll call the police."

Jake lowered himself into one of Jeanette's overstuffed chairs. "Good idea. I was going to call them myself, but you can save me the trouble."

Jeanette started toward the telephone, then stopped.

"Maybe I can understand that after so many years you didn't want all that work to lead to nothing," Nancy said. "But what about the animals? If the animal rights students hadn't shown up as you were about to burn down the lab, all those animals in there would have died. And the three students? You started that fire knowing they were in there."

Jeanette was trembling. "Didn't anyone notice what else was against the wall where the desk had burned?" she said, her voice breaking. "The fire alarms! I knew they'd go off right away. Nobody was going to get hurt."

"You were just lucky," Jake shot back.

"Those kids were crazy for showing up!" Jeanette cried. "How was I supposed to guess that? I had it all planned perfectly. It would have been blamed on the protesters, but no one in particular. But when I heard them, it was already too late. I had to leave, and the fire trucks were going to come. I thought no one would be injured."

"Except that's not what happened," Nancy said softly. "Someone was almost killed. And a lot of innocent people were hurt. Maybe not physically, but their lives were almost destroyed."

Jeanette's eyes glinted as she looked from Nancy to Jake. "You can't prove any of this!"

"That's where you're wrong," Jake said, on his feet again. "First, you changed the results—"

"Then the fire started in *your* office, on *your* desk," Nancy pointed out. "And conveniently included in the stuff that was burnt was all of *your* research work on HealthTech."

Jeanette shrugged. She glared at them hostilely.

"When I talked to you on Monday," Nancy continued, "you told me about seeing three people in the lab Sunday night, but how could you know how many people were there? The police didn't know it until Tuesday, and it wasn't in the paper!"

Jeanette folded her arms across her chest. "That's no proof. Maybe a lucky guess?"

"Give me a break," Jake said. "You wouldn't have known that unless you were there."

"And you were there because you work late at night and must have a key," Nancy pointed out. "You left the front door unlocked because you thought you wouldn't be long. But without your knowing it, you let Amy, Chaz, and Mike in."

Jeanette rolled her eyes, "Which proves what, you geniuses? Nothing, nothing, and nothing."

"You're forgetting one thing, Jeanette," Nancy said calmly and evenly. "The fire department knows what chemical started that fire. And the only samples of it in the entire state are sitting in your garage."

Jeanette started to speak, but she closed her mouth.

More unsurely now, she said, "I'll deny everything I said tonight. Nothing you have is hard evidence."

Nancy smiled and waved the folders. "Here's the motive." She pointed to the garage. "There's evidence, your desk is evidence—and you admitted everything to us, tonight, right here. We can testify."

"They won't believe you—" Jeanette said weakly.

"I wonder what HealthTech would say when we tell them everything we know and show them these folders," Nancy said. "When they find out that all their hopes for those drugs are based on lies. Your lies, Jeanette. Right here. In my hands."

Slowly lowering herself into a chair, Jeanette buried her face in her hands.

"The phone's right there," Nancy said. "You can make the call, or I can. But that call is going to be made—tonight."

CHAPTER 14

Okay, okay, ladies and ladies," Casey cried, prying open the bottle of sparkling grape juice Nancy had given her that morning and holding it high in the air. She looked around the lounge at all the curious expressions on the faces of her suitemates.

"I've gathered you all together because"— she paused—"Charley and I have an official announcement to make." Casey reached out, and Charley grabbed her fingers. Then he gave them a squeeze.

"Oh, my gosh, are they getting married?" Casey heard Liz Bader whisper.

"Charley and I," Casey began again, staring up at his beaming face, "are ..."

"Come on, come on, don't keep us in suspense!" Reva groaned.

Casey laughed. "Okay, okay. Charley and I are officially—engaged!"

Immediately, there were shrieks and cries in the suite's lounge. In seconds, Casey was surrounded.

"Congratulations!" Nancy cried, grabbing Casey and hugging her. "But we're so glad you're staying here with us."

"Now you're never going to get a date," Kara said.

"That's fine by me." Charley grinned, shaking his head at all the attention Casey was getting from her friends.

"Well, let's not ruin the party," Stephanie began, lazily raising a plastic glass in the air. "Here's a toast."

Casey turned to listen to her roommate. She was skeptical. It wasn't really a part of Steph's character to wish anybody well. Casey was actually curious to see if Stephanie could even do it at all. What would she consider good wishes, anyway?

Stephanie cleared her throat. "If you can make it through the back-stabbing world of Hollywood—through throngs of beautiful women and handsome jocks—through the rumors and lies of the ever-friendly, ever-watching tabloid press—and the two thousand miles between you . . ."

"Is this a toast?" Reva asked. "Or a monologue?"

"Then," Stephanie finished, smiling coolly, "I'm sure you'll have a wonderful marriage."

Casey gulped. It was quite a list—all the things that were going to make it hard for her and Charley to stay together. But then Casey felt Charley's warm hand on her back. "I love you," he whispered in her ear. Casey smiled.

"Thanks for the heartfelt sentiment, Steph," Casey joked. "Don't worry, we'll prove you right."

Nancy sat in the drawing room of the Vandenbrock mansion. She hoped this interview would go well, and that Mrs. Vandenbrock would prove a really interesting subject for her journalism profile. Nancy glanced around the room. Everything was so beautiful, and so expensive.

She'd been waiting for Mrs. Vandenbrock about five minutes when the ornate door swung open. A tall, extraordinarily beautiful woman walked in wearing a pale cream silk suit and a simple strand of pearls. Nancy noticed the glinting diamonds in her ears.

Mrs. Vandenbrock was probably in her fifties, Nancy guessed, but she looked much younger. She had blond hair rising back from her face into a high widow's peak, and piercing blue eyes. Her skin was smooth and creamy.

"So," Mrs. Vandenbrock said softly, "you're here to talk about my husband."

"Well, yes," Nancy said, her notebook poised on her knee. "From what I understand, your husband was a very important man in this town."

"Yes, he was," Mrs. Vandenbrock agreed, staring down at her hands. Nancy noticed she was holding them in small fists in her lap. "And he cared greatly for the university"—she inclined her head slightly—"which is why I've agreed to see you."

"I appreciate that," Nancy replied. "I think the best thing would be for me to just start asking you a few questions. Is that all right?"

Mrs. Vandenbrock nodded.

"I'd like to start off with your background, then," Nancy began. "Perhaps you can tell me a little bit about yourself. And where you met Mr. Vandenbrock—"

"Excuse me?" Mrs. Vandenbrock said. "Did you say *my* background?"

"Yes," Nancy replied. "If I'm going to do a complete profile of you, it's sort of important to know your history."

"I don't understand," Mrs. Vandenbrock said. "This is supposed to be about Wendell. I'm sorry. I will not answer any questions about myself." She reached behind her to pull a long braided cord. Instantly, the sour-looking man who'd let Nancy in appeared in the doorway.

Nancy's mouth fell open. Before she could speak, Mrs. Vandenbrock had risen from the couch and swept quickly from the room, without a backward glance. Then the butler took Nancy by the arm and propelled her out the front door. By the time Nancy had blinked, she was on the porch, the door closed behind her.

"What?" Nancy began, still struggling to get her bearings. "What? What just happened?"

Nancy turned around and looked back up at the huge house. She thought she saw a curtain falling back into place in one of the ground-floor windows.

"I guess that means the interview is over?" Nancy muttered, walking slowly back to her car.

"You know we're going to get you back, don't you?" Paul asked.

Bess grinned and lifted her face to the late-afternoon sun. The air was crisp and chill. It was a perfect day. Bess was bundled into her flannel-lined corduroy jacket.

"For some reason," she said cheerily, "my loss of sleep on Wednesday night hasn't seemed to affect my energy at all. In fact," she teased, "I've got a little bit more energy than I know what to do with. Perhaps I need to think of a way to work it off?"

Paul chuckled and hooked his arm through hers. He pulled her close as they walked along the path through the university quad.

"I've got a way for you to burn off some calories," he whispered, burrowing under her scarf and kissing her on the neck.

"Hey, guys!"

Bess and Paul stumbled to a halt. Bess turned, and her eyes popped! There was Leslie King with her new boyfriend, Nathan. But Bess almost wasn't sure it *was* Leslie. The straight brown hair was tousled from the wind. Leslie's cheeks had spots of pink in them. And she was wearing a heavy black wool sweater that looked eerily familiar.

"We're going to get some pizza subs from the Hot Truck," Leslie declared, as if she were announcing she'd just won the lottery. "And then we're going to the orchard to pick apples. After which, we'll be heading back to dinner at the Souvlaki House. Do you guys want to join us?"

"Sounds great," Bess said. "And thanks for inviting us, but we have to study."

"Unfortunately," Paul chimed in, "at the library."

"Study?" Leslie said, aghast. "On a day like today? Are you sure? Because we're going to have a lot of fun, and you're welcome to tag along."

"No, really." Bess smiled. "I'm sure all of it will be fun, though."

I wish *we* were going along instead of going to the library, she thought wistfully.

"Okay!" Leslie said enthusiastically. "Come on, Nathan, we've only got fifteen minutes to get to the Hot Truck!"

Nathan waved cheerily as Leslie pulled him off down the path.

"Wait a minute," Bess said, starting after Leslie and Nathan. "There was something really weird about her just now."

"Yeah," Paul agreed. "She started out as the Ice Cube Roommate from Hell, and now she's turned into the Dating Roommate from Hell."

"No!" Bess cried, suddenly realizing what had bothered her. "I mean, yes, but that's not what I noticed."

"Well, what is it?" Paul asked.

"This may sound unbelievable," Bess said, shaking her head. "But she's wearing some of my clothes again!"

Stephanie was having a dream. In the dream, she stumbled down the street, her tattered skirt tangling around her legs. Her bare feet were numb after walking so far in the crisp fall air. Finally, up ahead, she saw the faint yellow sign swaying in the wind.

There it was! Stephanie sighed, almost crying with joy. She wiped her greasy, unwashed hair from her eyes. Chez Cher—the most expensive restaurant in the world.

"What's the time?" Stephanie cried out, grabbing a passerby in a long dark coat.

"Five to seven," he muttered, shrugging her off and scurrying away.

Five minutes! Stephanie was frantic. Five minutes until her reservation. The reservation she'd waited years to get.

Stephanie stumbled to the window. There was her table—a beautiful, intimate table for two. And there was her date—the Incredibly Gorgeous Man! Stephanie almost died with thankfulness. She turned from the window and hurried to the front door.

"I'm sorry, madam," the maitre d' said, stopping her before she could enter. He looked at her clothes and wrinkled his nose. "But only those with reservations allowed."

"But I have one," Stephanie cried happily. "Stephanie Keats, just check and see."

The maitre d' punched her name into the computer, then after waiting a second, turned to her.

"Sorry," he said, his smile cruel, "but you are over the limit. No cards," he said, starting to laugh. "No clothes, no money."

Stephanie looked around desperately. Just over the maitre d's shoulder, she could see the Incredibly Gorgeous Man at her table. He lifted his wrist and checked his watch. Then he sighed, disgusted, and rose to leave.

"No!" Stephanie cried, reaching out to him.

"No! Oh, no!" Stephanie moaned, burying her face in her silk-covered pillow. Stephanie woke with a start. She opened her eyes and shuddered. Her little afternoon catnap had turned into a full-fledged nightmare. It had seemed so real. Especially the part about her having an Incredibly Gorgeous Man as a date. But the rest of it— Stephanie shivered.

I can't live without money! What am I going to do? Stephanie tried to block the idea that came floating into her mind.

Suddenly, she sat up, her eyes wide. Is it possible? she asked herself. Is this what my father wanted all along?

Stephanie shook her head. "But it can't be," she said out loud. "I don't want to get a job!"

"I can't believe this was really Gail's idea," Nancy said as she typed furiously into her computer.

"No kidding," Jake agreed. "This is going to be a great story: Falsely accused of arson and racing against the clock to clear themselves and solve the crime."

"Side-by-side personal accounts," Nancy added.

They were writing up the story about the

radical animal activists, the fire, and Jeanette Rigaud.

Their article told how Jeanette had lost her job offer with HealthTech and also how she was looking at real jail time for fraud, property damage, and reckless endangerment.

Nancy glanced over to sneak a peek at her boyfriend. She couldn't explain the way her heart lurched as she stared at Jake hard at work.

Well, Nancy realized, reading over her work, she and Jake had gone through their first real challenge as a couple. And it had been quite a crisis—threatening to break them up, as well as get them kicked out of school.

But we weathered the storm, Nancy realized. We've started a whole new partnership.

"So what about this byline?" Jake grinned in delight as the mock-up pages of Monday's edition were tossed onto their desk. "Take a look, Drew," he teased. "It's there in print: 'Jake Collins and Nancy Drew.' "

Nancy reached over, snatched the mock-up from him, and studied it thoughtfully.

"Only one problem," she pointed out. "It should say Nancy Drew and Jake Collins."

"That's cute." Jake chuckled indulgently. "But I *am* the senior reporter on this team."

"Oh, I'm sure it was just an alphabetical decision," Nancy stated.

Jake stood up from his chair.

"Don't think you're going to bully me into playing second fiddle," Nancy warned as Jake stepped closer. "And there's no way I'm going to let you ride *my* name to stardom." She gasped as Jake grabbed her around the waist.

"Oh, I wouldn't dream of it," Jake whispered, catching her face in his hands. "I know I've got my work cut out for me. Just keeping up with you is going to be a challenge."

"Don't worry," Nancy said as Jake's lips lowered to hers. "I'll slow down for you every once in a while."

NEXT IN NANCY DREW ON CAMPUS™:

Nancy's suitemate Eileen O'Connor just can't seem to keep up with her friends. Her social life has gone south: no dates, no guys, no fun! Football player Emmet Lehman could change all that. Sure, nobody's perfect, and maybe it's a big mistake, but he's smart, he's handsome, and he's asked Eileen to the upcoming party at her sorority. Nancy, too, is looking for answers . . . to two questions, both related to a campus film festival: one, the truth behind an unsolved, three-decades-old crime—a scandalous case in which a movie ended in murder; and two, the reason for her attraction to one of the festival's organizers. His name is Terry Schneider, and he looks exactly like Ned . . . in *Campus Exposures,* Nancy Drew on Campus #13.